GEORGE W. MACPH … of
Skye. He has follo … n
through generatio … e
of the best known traditional storytellers in Scotland. George's storytelling technique is both memorable and distinctive, capable of captivating any audience, young or old, all over the world.

George began collecting stories at the age of three, and has amassed an impressive repertoire of stories from all over Scotland, ranging from the heroes of Celtic folklore to the mythical and fantastical creatures of Scottish myth. He has told his stories in many countries world-wide, including France, Germany, Malta, Thailand, Spain and England. In 1997 he opened the Commonwealth Heads of State Convention in Edinburgh with one of his stories.

As well as telling stories, George has published an historical account of John Macpherson, *Skye Martyr*, and two books of traditional stories, *North West Skye* and *Highland Myths and Legends*. He has also had published many articles in papers and magazines, both prose and poetry, on a variety of subjects, and has contributed to Cuillin FM, the radio station for Skye. A participant in the Edinburgh Storytelling Festival for ten years, he also organises the annual Skye and Lochalsh Storytelling Festival, bringing to Scotland the storytelling traditions of countries such as France and Spain.

A wearer of the kilt, either in its modern mode or in its ancient and traditional form, the philimore, he believes that stories should entertain and that the great stories of the oral tradition should not be altered but should be told as they were learned.

Luath Storyteller Series

Celtic Sea Stories

GEORGE W MacPHERSON

Luath Press Limited

EDINBURGH

www.luath.co.uk

First Published 2009
Reprinted 2013
This Edition 2016
Reprinted 2017
Reprinted 2018

ISBN 978-1-910021-86-6

The paper used in this book is recyclable. It is made from low chlorine pulps produced in a low energy, low emissions manner from renewable forests.

The publisher acknowledges subsidy from

towards the publication of this volume.

Printed and bound by
CPI Antony Rowe, Chippenham

Typeset in 10.5 point Sabon by
3btype.com

Illustrations by Alice Gamper

contents

Preface 9

The Dark Doctor – *An Dotair Dhubh* 13
Real Mist 19
The Whale of Mull 21
The Greenock Lass 25
The Cave of Death – *Uamh Nan Bas* 31
The Battle of the Spoiled Dykes – *La Mille Garaidh* 37
Ramasaig – The Three Witches 43
The White Cow of Greshornish 47
Blar Breacan Phuill – The Blood Spot Flower 51
The Farmer's Wife – *Bean Tuathanach* 55
The Girl from under the Sea – *Cala Lochlanaich* 65
The Old Man of Skye – *Bodach Sgith* 71
The Silver Chanter 75
Annag MacCruimen 79
One of Those Who Search Always 83
Sgiath's Gift to Love – *Tiodhlaic Sgiath an Gaol* 87
The Cup of Healing – *Cupan Beatha* 91
The Sound of the Surge of the Sea – *An Ataireachd Ard* 111

The Three Feathers – *Na Tri h'Itean* 117
The Last Great Clan Battle 123
Brandon the Navigator 129
Hector the Fisherman – *Eachan An't Iasgair* 135
Amadan Domhnallach – MacDonald's Fool 143
The Boat – *Am Bata* 147
The Minister and the Evils of Drink 151
The People from Under the Sea – *An Lochlannaich* 153
Lochlannaich – The People from below the Sea 159
The Flying Barrel 165
Mermaids – *Maighdean Mhara* 167
Seamus and the Monster 171
The Ship that Died for Love 175
The Loch of the Grey Wolf – *Loch Madadh Glaseachd* 179
The Factor of Kilchoan 183

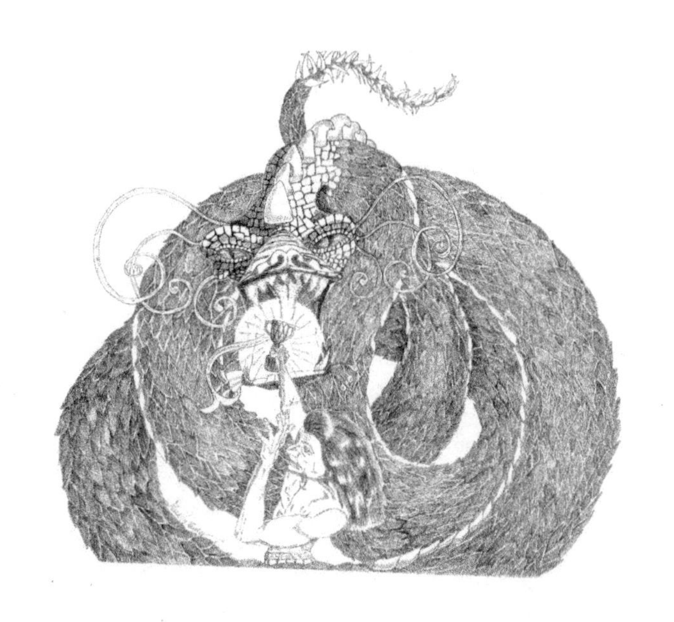

preface

HIS BOOK IS like my previous books, especially so *Highland Myths and Legends*, in that through them I try to preserve some of the stories told to me by many persons of varying ages and areas.

Several of the stories were given to me on the condition that if I told or published them the name of the teller would not be connected to them. In fact, some were very insistent on such a promise before they told the stories to me. I have tried to be faithful to their wishes even though many of them are 'Past the Change' as it was called earlier on; what is now known as death.

One of the reasons I have tried to maintain this promise is that I discovered there was a belief in the very old Celtic tradition that if a story was recorded in any way whilst the teller was telling it, then part of the spirit of both story and teller died with it. Even my own father would not allow his stories to be recorded and if he thought a shorthand writer, or tape recorder, or any such thing was in range, he would refuse to tell and remain silent till he was sure the coast was clear.

These stories carry in them the culture and way of life of whatever age they are set, whether ancient or modern, and in some cases it is difficult to differentiate between them.

When a story is passed to one it brings with it a duty and privilege to be true to the story and allow the natural rhythm of it to carry as you tell. It is the story that counts, not the teller. I hope in this book I have achieved that aim and that in written form I have managed to preserve the natural rhythm of the story and readers know it is the story and not the author. These are stories of the sea and its people, An Lochlannaich, and their descendants who carry its spirit with them wherever they wander.

Throughout my life I have been lucky in that people have confided stories to me and stories have happened around me, just waiting for their time to be told. I hope this continues and is reflected in the book.

I have had great help in the production of this book and especially so from Kati Waitzmann, who with great patience typed the stories from my dictation – and did it with a smile. My thanks to her. My thanks go also to the publishers, who encouraged me and showed patience in my slow production of the manuscripts.

My thanks also to my wife and family, who listened to me telling the stories many times and did not pour cold water on my efforts too often.

Above all my thanks to all the friends and relations who passed stories to me over the last seventy years, and even the odd enemy who did the same.

Seoras Macpherson
George W. Macpherson 2009

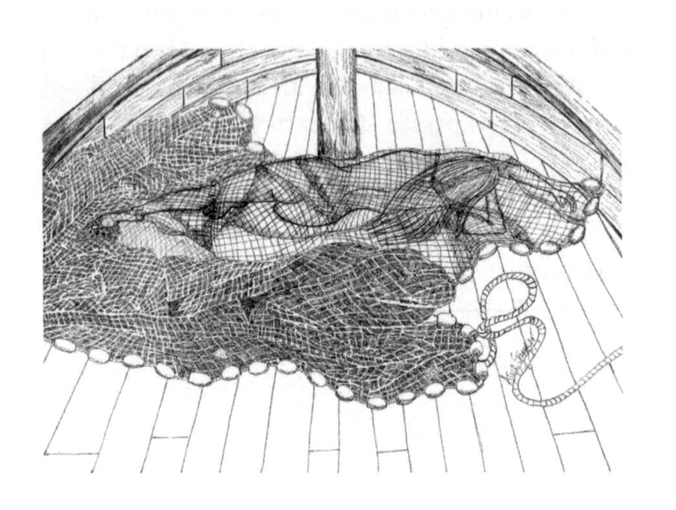

the dark doctor – *an dotair dhubh*

IN THE FURTHEST WEST PART of Skye, in a place now called Glendale there lived a woman and her son. She was very poorly off. She had a small house and a little plot of land. On the plot of land she grew some potatoes, a little oats and she had a goat that she milked. But her pride and joy was her son. He was everything to her, but the son was a strange boy. He would wander down by the shore, listen to the sound of the waves and always he looked as if he was searching for something. He was never one with the other children and people would say to his mother, 'Oh, he will grow out of it. He'll grow out of it and help you on the croft. He'll help you with all your work.'

But the boy grew older and he made no sign of wanting to help with the work. Still all he wanted to do was wander down by the shore, dream his dreams and search for whatever it was he was searching for – which even he didn't know what it was.

But then, one day he was down by the shore he saw bobbing out in the sea something strange. At first he thought it was a wrack of seaweed that had been carried in by the tide but when he looked more he saw it was not seaweed and he could not decide what this object was. So he waited there at the shore to see what it could be. The sea tossed it in closer and closer until it landed in the sand at his feet. He looked at it and it was a strange object. It was like a triangle made of wood with two long sides and a short side. And then between the short side and one of the long sides there were strings. When he picked it up and touched the strings, they sang. He picked it up and carried it up to the house and when his mother saw it, she told him to put it back into the sea as it was probably an evil gift from the fairies of the sea, the little people below the sea, who gave only evil gifts. But the boy would not listen to her. He placed his fingers upon the strings again and heard the sounds they made. But the music that was in his heart he could not put through his fingers to the strings and he tried very hard. Every day after that, he went out to try out the sound of the strange thing but he could not get the music out of it that he wanted. And his mother saw him striving there and felt the song was in him but he could not pour out the music of his heart.

To do the best for her son she went and saw the Dark Doctor; the Doctor whom some said was in league with the devil. Some said he *was* the devil, but she went to see him and said to him what her son had and asked the Dark Doctor to give the gift to her son, hoping he would be able to get the music from his heart into the strings, into his fingers.

The Doctor said, 'Oh, I can do that. That is no problem. But what can you give me in return?'

And the woman thought, 'as I have very little, nothing.' She replied, 'You can have me if you want.'

And the Dark Doctor laughed at her. 'Why would I want an old wrinkled crone like you?', says he. 'What good would that do me?'

'Well', she said. 'I don't think I have anything else I can give, but whatever I can give I will if you'll give my son this gift.'

And the Dark Doctor said, 'Well, if you will promise to give me your soul when I come for it, I will do this for your son.'

The woman agreed. And when she had done so the Dark Doctor said to her, 'The thing that your son has is called the clarsach. And already I have fulfilled my part of the bargain and you must fulfil yours.'

The woman went back to the croft and there was her son sitting, his fingers ranging across the strings of the clarsach and from it poured music, beautiful music, such as never had been heard before. The woman knew that the Dark Doctor had indeed given her wish to her son.

The son kept playing the clarsach and grew better and better. His music grew greater and greater. Nobody had ever heard such music. But then the son noticed that his mother was looking strange and was feeling strange. She was not as she had been. And the son said to his mother, 'What is it?' 'Why are you like this?' He kept asking her. Eventually, the mother told him what she had done.

The boy was aghast. He thought this was a terrible thing altogether and he went to the Dark Doctor and asked him to take away the gift of music that had been given him, and set free his mother from the promise she had made. But the Dark Doctor just laughed and said,

'No. We have made a pact and it will be carried out and you will have that gift forever. I, however, will have your mother's soul.'

The boy went back to the croft and continued to play the clarsach. But now there was sadness in his music, as had not been there before; soulfulness, a haunting sound. And the time came when the Dark Doctor arrived at the door and demanded the soul of the mother, and the mother died there and then. Afterwards the boy played on, and the music that he played now was wonderful; wonderful, beautiful, magical music. Music nobody had ever heard before. Music, that rang out all through the world. But there was a sad haunting in the music and always a tremendous sadness. And this was the origin of music. And the sadness is there still to this day, for if anyone plays the clarsach, no matter what tune they play, there is always behind it the haunting sadness that no one knows where it came from.

Real mist

WHEN I WAS JUST a young bit of a lad, there was an old man down in the glen and his name was Neil. Old Neil he was called, Neil Seinn. Old Neil had a good boat which required four men to pull the oars. Neil himself was just beyond pulling at an oar then, but four of us young lads in the glen would go down, take the boat down with him and row out with Neil sitting at the stern and steering with a sweep. We would go and we would fish. And at that time it was easy to catch fish. You could fill the boat in just an hour or two's fishing without much bother at all.

We were rowing out across Moonen Bay, well past the Neistpoint Lighthouse, when all of a sudden the mist came down; thick mist. We decided it would be better if we headed back. That was fine, and the mist was getting thicker but it wasn't a great bother to us because we could hear the foghorn of Neistpoint Lighthouse booming out. We followed the sound of it quite happily. Then the old Neil started to talk.

He said to us. 'Well boys, you know this isn't

a real mist at all. When I was a young man we had real mist. This is nothing. And we did not have a Lighthouse to steer by then either.'

Which was absolutely true, because the Lighthouse was only built in 1908.

He said, 'We used to go out in the mist and we would go out and the mist would come down. But this day that I remember well, the mist came down and it came down thick; thick and heavy. It was so thick and heavy that you could cut it into slabs.'

'Ach yes, that would be right Neil', said we. 'That would be right, aye?'

'Well', said Neil. 'It's right enough, I tell you boys, and the boat we were in, it had a mast, so we could sail her as well as row her. I was the youngest and the lightest of the crew, so eventually I was told to go and climb the mast. Maybe I could see over the top of the mist, which does sometimes happen, that you could see over the top of the mist.

'Well you know boys', he said. 'I climbed up the mast and looked to the North and to the South and to the East and to the West and all I could see was mist. Not even a bit of headland or anything. And you know this boys, when I climbed back down, the boat was gone.'

the whale of mull

ON THE ISLAND OF MULL there is a long peninsula known as Oa, the Oa of Mull. It runs from Bunnessan down to Fionnphort, where there is now the crossing to Iona. Quite a few years ago this peninsula was dependent entirely on itself for produce from the sea and from the land. There wasn't a great deal of land so the main thing was to fish from the sea. The fish would be caught during the summer weather, the good weather, and it would be smoked, salted and stored for food over the winter. If the people would not make use of that they would die of starvation.

One year the crops had been poor, what little there was of them, and what made things even worse, the fishing had been very bad indeed. When winter came in the people realised that they had not enough food to last them over the complete winter. They started as best they could by reducing the rations but by midwinter they were already out of food and starting to starve.

There was an old man with his two sons at Bunnessan and they were reckoned to be the best fishers of all. They said if a window would come up in the weather, a small break in the weather, regardless of the risk, they would go out on their boat and try to catch some fish to help them through the winter. Although it would not feed the whole of Oa, it would help. Soon enough there came about a small break in the weather and the old man and his two sons, true to their word, launched their boat and rowed out to sea. They rowed out and they fished for the whole of the winter's day but they caught not one single fish. Eventually as night was coming in fast they realised they have to turn back to Bunnessan. As they were turning the boat they saw a whale in the horizon, a whale lying like a bank of mist on the surface.

The old man said to his two boys, 'Well now boys, if we could catch that whale and get it ashore we could feed every person on the whole of Oa of Mull for the whole of the winter.'

The two boys looked at their father. 'Oh, don't be so daft. Look at it!' they said. 'It is far bigger than us and our boat combined, far bigger. We could never do that.'

'Ach yes, you are right enough,' said the old man. But he said, 'We will turn around before we head back to the land, just to see what it's like.' So they rowed out to see the great whale and started to row around it. As they came to the head of the whale all of a sudden its mouth opened wide and with a great gulp down went the boat, the old man and his two sons into the stomach of the whale. And there they were down in the whale's stomach, still in their boat. The two sons looked at the old man and said, 'Look! What have you got us into now? How are we ever to get out of this?'

'Oh well', said the old man. 'It's a bit of a bad position right enough and we'll need to think what we can do.'

Then he took out his sharp knife. For every Muileach, every man from Mull, carries a very sharp knife because of Fraoch, but that is another story altogether.

The old man took out his knife and he leant over one side of the boat to cut a hole in the side of the whale. He leant to the other side of the boat to cut a hole in the other side of the whale.

'Now', he said to the boys. 'You put your oar through that hole and you', he said to the other son, 'put your oar out through the other hole. When I tell you to start rowing you row as hard as you can. When I tell you to pull hard to the right you pull hard to the right. If I tell you to pull hard to the left you pull hard to the left.'

So the two boys did as they were bidden. They started to row as hard as they could. The old man told them to pull to the right or the left as he fancied and they rowed and they rowed and they rowed till their backs felt as if they were breaking. Their hands, even though they were used to rowing, were bleeding. Then just as they were about to give up the whale suddenly run aground. When it run aground it gave a great belch and out of its mouth shot the old man and his two sons and the boat. They landed on the shore and there they were on the shore of Bunnessan, just in front of the Argyle Arms Hotel.

That whale fed all the people of whole Oa of Mull for the rest of the winter.

I first heard this story in Ardnamurchan and it was told in one particular place in Ardnamurchan, I heard about it in the 1940s from a grand uncle. Then much later on, in about the '70s, I heard the story told by a Mr MacKiechan on Mull. He of course had the story placed in Mull. The version told here is a much compressed version and a combination of the two.

the Greenock lass

UITE A NUMBER of years ago there was a girl on the Isle of Skye. She was not well looked upon in Skye at all. She was too much like a boy. She was a big strong girl. She took part in the boys' sports rather than the girls', and because of this she was ostracised. People turned their back on her and didn't talk to her.

The girl decided, if this is the way of things, she would leave Skye and go and seek her fortune somewhere else. So she left Skye and she walked down south. She walked for many days until eventually she arrived in a fishing town, in Greenock. Now at this time Greenock was a very busy fishing town and also a very busy seaport. The girl watched the goings-on and saw how the ships were manned. She thought to herself, 'Perhaps I could get involved in this and make my fortune, by sailing out say to the West Indies, bringing back a cargo and selling it off. But I can't afford a ship.'

So she thought for a while about this. Then she bought some men's clothes. She strapped her womanly parts down tight and put on the men's clothes. She went and got a berth on a sailing ship.

The ship sailed from Greenock to Jamaica. When they got to Jamaica, the girl, because of her ability and her willingness to work, had made herself a favourite with the skipper. When they got to Jamaica the girl asked the skipper if she could buy some stuff herself as her pay, and take it back with her to sell it to some other ports. The skipper agreed to this. The girl got some goods and sold them in a different port and made money on them. She did this for several voyages. And always the home port was Greenock and they went back there. Greenock became the second home of the girl.

After a few years of this, the skipper discovered that this man whom he had sailed with so regularly was not a man at all, but a woman. He was very taken with this. He and the Greenock lass got together and became married. The skipper owned three ships. Now the Greenock lass started to get money in.

But the happiness did not last long, for the skipper was killed in an accident on board ship and she was now his widow. But all his money and all his ships came to her. She saw now the way of making a fortune. She worked hard. She was the skipper of her own ship, she sailed the others at different times and she managed them all. She added to the fleet some seven ships. The new ones were built at Cairds Yard in Greenock for now she regarded Greenock as her home. Then one day, on a trip to the West Indies, she overheard some of the crew talking in Gaelic. When she heard this all the things that she had suppressed, all the thoughts of Skye, came back to her; the thoughts and dreams of her own homeland.

Hearing the Gaelic spoken in this way made her heart ache. When the ships came back she sold the lot, sold them all down in Greenock. With the money she got she travelled back to Skye, but now she travelled in a horse drawn carriage, well attended. When she came to Skye, many of the people she had known were still there. She made herself known to them and they were amazed that this girl they had laughed at and sneered at was now a very wealthy woman.

But she saw that although they now praised her and spoke to her, they didn't do this because they really thought well of her. They did it because she was wealthy. So she decided that Skye was not really for her. She bought a house in Skye and turned it into a hotel, one of the earliest hotels in Skye, but she only ran it for a short time and then left again.

She went with her horse drawn carriage back to Greenock, which was now her home. She set up and built the big house in what is now the West End area in Greenock. She gave the house a Gaelic name just to remember where her roots were, and occasionally friends from Skye would come down and visit her there. But in spite of all her wealth, in spite of the wealth she has brought herself, she was lonely, for she was alone there. Nothing, not even a child she had to keep her company. But then again the wheels of fortune turned.

One day she met a man, a man who was not young and not yet old. A man who had himself had a hard time throughout his life. He loved her, not for her wealth and for her houses, but for herself. The two of them married and they lived on in Greenock and from Jamaica they brought three Jamaican babies. They lived in Greenock and grew up in Greenock as a family. They were known in Greenock as the 'black and whites' because of course the Jamaican children were black and the father and mother white. But no notice was ever taken of this. They were all equal with one another, and accepted as such by the good people of Greenock.

the cave of death – *uamh nan bas*

OW IT CAME ABOUT that MacLeod of MacLeod's son, the younger son, was at sea in a galley with his men. A great storm came up and they were driven before it. There was a great need to find shelter and the first shelter they found was the island of Eigg. They managed to get their galley ashore and expected, as was the custom throughout the highlands, that although the people on Eigg were the MacDonalds they would give them hospitality and would let them go safely on their way. Instead of this the people in Eigg, the MacDonalds – they were also from Rum and Muck, gathered in Eigg at that time – took the MacLeods and killed most of them, after torturing them. They took the young son of MacLeod, tortured him, castrated him as part of the torture, then they took his mutilated body and put it aboard a boat; an old, raggedy, ramshackled boat that they thought would sink quite quickly. They tied him into it and let it go off to the sea.

By some freak of the winds and the currents the boat was carried back to Dunvegan in Skye, where his father and his brothers found the mutilated body of young MacLeod. He was not yet quite dead and he told them what had happened; how the MacDonalds of Eigg and Rum and Muck had treated him and his men this way. MacLeod of MacLeod, upon hearing this, was furious. He said, 'The MacDonalds shall pay for this.'

He made ready three galleys of men. He sent his best and most fearsome warriors and said, 'Sail for Eigg!'

The people of Eigg saw the galleys coming from a distance, and the people of Rum and Muck were again with them at that time. They realised they could not withstand the force that MacLeod had with him but on Eigg there is a great cave and the people decided they would hide in the cave, every man, woman and child. They made their way to the entrance of the cave, which is very hard to find even now. They went into the cave and pulled brushwood across the mouth of it until it was well hidden.

When the MacLeods reached the island there was no one there. They searched all over the island but not one person did they find. Eventually they decided that the people must have fled before they came, so they started to sail away in their galleys. As they sailed away, a shower of snow came across and one of the MacLeods looking back saw a figure of a man appearing on Eigg. It was then they realised that they must have been tricked in some manner and they headed back to Eigg again.

Now the man had seen the galleys going away and run back to the cave, but with the shower of snow he left his footprints on the ground. The MacLeods, following the footprints, found they were leading into the cave. They shouted into the cave to the MacDonalds and asked them to come out and fight but the MacDonalds refused to do this, for they knew that if the MacLeods tried to come in through the entrance of the cave they could kill them easily one at a time. The entrance was a tight passage and only one person at a time could go in through it so they felt quite safe in the cave.

William the chief of MacLeod ordered his men to gather together all the brushwood and every piece of burnable stuff they could find and bring it all to the mouth of the cave.

His men did as they were told. One of the brothers of the man who had been killed by the MacDonalds on Eigg shouted into the cave before the fire was lit, for he knew that in the cave was a man who had saved his life on one occasion. So he shouted for the man and the man answered him. He offered the man his life and safety if he would come out. The man in the cave replied, 'Will you promise it also for my wife and my children?'

But MacLeod was not willing to do that. 'In that case', the man replied, 'I will remain here in the cave with my wife and children.'

The brushwood was piled into the mouth of the cave and lit by the MacLeods.

Every single soul in the cave was killed. One or two of the MacDonalds tried to rush through the flames, to save themselves, and were killed by the spears and swords of the MacLeods until eventually there was not one single living soul of the MacDonalds left on the whole of Eigg. The MacLeods left the bodies lying in the cave, went back to their galleys and sailed back to Dunvegan but the younger son of the MacLeods who had offered the man the chance to escape, and then refused it because the offer included not the wife and the children; he was known from that time on as William the Vicious, and he was one of the most cruel and hard hearted MacLeod chiefs who ever lived.

The cave is still there to be seen if you have the fortune of finding the hidden entrance.

The Battle of the Spoiled Dykes – *La Mille Garaidh*

AFTER THE MACLEODS had carried out their massacre in Eigg, the MacDonalds came back to the island and discovered what had happened to every person on the island. The MacDonalds of the islands swore vengeance on the MacLeods and in order to have it they set sail with a strong fleet of galleys heading for Skye.

As the galleys sailed past Dunvegan Head, there was a man called Fionnlaidh na Plaide Bhan, Finlay of the White Plaid, out fishing with four of his companions and they saw the galleys of MacDonald heading towards Dunvegan. Finlay and his companions went back to the shore as fast as they could to warn MacLeod. But one of the galleys came after them and as fast as they rowed the galley was catching up on them. Finlay and his men jumped ashore at Galtrigill and went as fast as they could towards Borreraig. They were running for all

they were worth but the galley of Macdonald
was close behind them and men leapt from it
and were following them fast. Now the four
companions of Finlay knew that there was a
ruin of a small Broch to the left up in the
headland. They thought if they went up there,
there might be a way to hide in the ruins.
They turned and went to the ruins, but
MacDonald's men saw them and came after
them. The four companions were slain in the
remains of the Broch. Finlay of the White Plaid
ran on and on until he reached Uiginish.
In Uiginish he put his hands to his mouth
and he gave such a bellow across the water
that he roused the sentries in Dunvegan Castle.
He bellowed across at them that the galleys of
MacDonald were coming, and that they looked
as though they had changed their course and
were going in to Waternish.

The chief of MacLeod was away somewhere
so the chieftainess roused the clan. She sent
around the fiery cross and gathered around her
as many men as she could but in the meantime
the galleys of Macdonald had landed at Trumpan
in Waternish. It was a Sunday and all the
MacLeods of that area were in the church

at Trumpan. When the MacDonalds came up on the church they set fire to it for the roof was thatched and burned easily. The MacLeods were trapped inside the church and when they tried to run out of the doors and windows they were killed – except for one woman who forced her way through a very narrow slit window at one end of the church. It was so narrow that in forcing her way through it she tore off her breasts and she started to run back towards Dunvegan. When she was part way there she met the men of MacLeod led by the chieftainess hastening as fast as they could towards Trumpan. Before the woman died she told them of what had happened and they charged on even faster.

When they reached Trumpan they were too late to save the people in the church. Although they were smaller in number than the MacDonalds, they attacked the MacDonalds with great vim and vigour, led by their chieftainess. A great battle ensued but it looked as though the MacDonalds, because of their greater numbers, were to overpower the MacLeods. At the moment it seemed that all was lost for the MacLeods, the standard bearer of MacLeods unfurled a flag; the fairy flag. From out of nowhere appeared a great host of armed men who rushed upon the MacDonalds and hacked and slew them.

The MacDonalds turned and ran to their galleys, down on the shore at Ardmore, but they made a mistake when they pulled the galleys up on to the shore. The tide had been going out and now their galleys, except for one, were stranded there on the shore. Some of them managed to get into the one galley which was still able to sail and they set off. The rest of the MacDonald men were trapped down at Ardmore and the battle that ensured there was known, and is still known, as *The Battle of the Spoiled Dykes*. So many MacDonalds were slain that they could not think of digging graves for them so the MacLeods laid them along below a dyke which stood along the shore They put the stones of the dyke on top of the slain bodies and this is why the battle was called The Battle of the Spoiled Dykes (or Spoiled Walls).

The one galley which had got away was heading into the open sea and they could not catch it, but the chieftainess of the MacLeod was not going to allow it to escape and she called in a witch. She was a witch from

Waternish. The witch put a curse, an incantation, on the galley, so it would never reach the shores of the Western Isles. As the galley passed Neist Point, suddenly, from nowhere came a huge giant wave which engulfed the galley and broke it into bits, and the few MacDonalds who had managed to escape with the galley were drowned off Neist Point. So every MacDonald who had taken part in the raid was slain in one way or another.

Ramasaig – the three witches

RAMASAIG WAS AT one time very famous because of three witches who once lived there. At a certain time of the year, at the right turn of the moon, those three witches would go down to the bay at Ramasaig and there they would make certain incantations as the setting sun turned the water red. They would make the incantations and dance there and walk naked into the sea, then out of the sea would come three red rams. The witches would take the rams up to where they lived in Ramasaig. The rams would serve certain amounts of ewes, and in the following spring there would be red lambs. These red lambs were highly sought and very precious, for the coat on them served rich dark crimson red, and red of course was a colour that was very hard to get in a dye from the plants. And so the local people roundabout Ramasaig always sought to persuade the witches to have their rams serve some of their sheep. But the witches would only do this to people who had been kind to them, who had helped them in some way, so there were very few of the red sheep born.

The other thing was that after a year, after the first shearing, the red disappeared from their coats and they were back to just ordinary sheep.

After a while it was noted by the people roundabout that the witches brought these rams up and did not hold them in any way. The rams were allowed to just go back into the sea when they wanted to.

The people thought now, if they could perhaps capture one of these rams when they were making their way back into the sea, to detain it inside walled enclosures so the ram could not get out, they could then keep the ram for years and have many red sheep. And the greed for the red wool was too much for them so they decided they would do this. The following autumn when the rams came out of the sea again the people waited. When the rams started to go back to the sea in November time the people trapped one of the rams and put it in an enclosure, hoping to get all those red sheep from it. But the witches soon discovered this and they were absolutely enraged. They worked with their magic and destroyed the walls of the enclosure. The ram ran out into the sea and after this the sheep of the crofters of the people roundabout, who had been sired by the rams, all of them rushed to the sea and died there.

And so for greed the people of Ramasaig lost what they had in red wool and the red rams of Ramasaig were never seen again, although often times people tried to breed from certain sheep in the hope they might restore again the red of the rams of Ramasaig.

This story came to me from three different sources; two very elderly ladies and one elderly man. Each of them told the story slightly differently and I tried to accumulate the three versions into one here, although there was very little difference between the stories to be honest. The persons who told me the stories, at the time they told it were in their late 80s and late 90s. None of them wanted their names associated with the story. Each of them claimed that the story had happened at the time of their great grandparents.

the white cow of Greshornish

AT GRESHORNISH AT this time there lived a man on a very small patch of ground. He didn't even own a cow and had to beg for milk from neighbours. Although he was in such a bad way of living he always hoped that someday, somehow, his life would improve, that he would become not perhaps wealthy in the sense of the world, but having enough that he and the family he hoped to have could live comfortably.

He was a very honest man in all his dealings. He followed the rituals right down to the little people and the druids. When he would go to the shore to gather seaweed as fertilizer for his little bit of land he would leave an offering to the gods of the sea, to Honi especially, the god of the seaweed. And if he was in the hills cutting peat or doing something similar, he would leave an offering to the little people of the land. At the right time of the year he would carry out the rituals for that particular time. He was not alone in doing this at that time because people did carry out the rituals, but he was very particular in it.

Now one day, as he was down at the shore in Greshornish gathering seaweed, he heard the mooing of a cow in distress. He went to see what it was and further along the shore he came upon a beautiful white cow laying over on its side. There was a rock which appeared to have rolled over and landed on the cow's hind legs and pinned it down. The man was sorry for the plight of the cow and with great difficulty he managed to lever the rock away from its legs and allow the cow to stand. He headed back to his piece of ground but discovered when he did that the white cow was following along behind him. He and the cow arrived home and the man, seeing that the cow was full of calf, gave it some food to eat and then went out to his neighbours to see who had lost a cow. But none had, nor had they heard of anybody else who had lost a cow. So the man went back home and

not long after the cow calved, a beautiful white calf. The cow had plenty of milk, so the man had milk for himself and he had the calf to sell at the autumn sales.

When he sold the calf he bought more land and so it went on, each year the cow would calf and the man would sell the calf until eventually he had enough land and enough milk that he could keep more of the calves instead of selling them on. His herd grew to a very good herd and always he would sell off some of the calves every year. Now being a man of some means he got himself a wife and he had a good large family, fine strong sons and healthy daughters. As the man was getting older, the sons and daughters started to take over more of the work about the farm. Some of the daughters got married off. Some of the sons had wives. But then they started pestering their father, for the old man would not sell the white cow that had come to him from the sea, that he had found while gathering seaweed. Although she was old now, she was still a good cow and gave good calves. But the young folk kept on at him, 'Oh, you should be selling the old beast now. After all, we are selling so many of her calves and so many of the medium beasts, that really we are not doing ourselves any credit by keeping her.'

But the old man would not have it. That cow

was to be kept and the cow was kept and kept till the old man fell very ill. The sons and daughters and the family in general decided now was the time, when the old man was not well, to sell the white cow. But when she was put together with the other ones which were going to be taken to the market, the white cow led all the other cattle in a great rush, in a stampede away from the farm and back down towards the sea, and as she went all the other descendants of her at the farm followed her. The whole complete herd dived into the sea of Greshornish, swam out into the sea, disappeared and were never ever seen again. The white cows of Greshornish were gone forever. And from that time on the fortunes of that family went down and down.

This story was told to me by an old man in Edinbane who has been dead many years now, but he locked it in with a clearance of Diubaig at Greshornish.

Blar Breacan Phuill – the Blood Spot Flower

MANY YEARS AGO when the persecution of the Christians in Israel had reached a very great height, St Andrew decided he would need to do something to preserve the Christian ideal, for he felt that it could perhaps be wiped out and the ideals lost.

To this end he took one of his followers and together they stood on the stone of destiny, *Jacob's Pillow*. They stood on the stone and the stone lifted into the air and carried them out over the land and across the sea. St Andrew had taken with him roots of a small flower, a flower which grew at the spot where Jesus was crucified. This flower had been plain yellow but, when the Roman soldier thrust his spear into the side of Jesus and droplets of blood had splashed from Jesus' side onto the flower, the flower had become spotted with blood. And so it had remained and it was known as the Blood Spot Flower or, in the Highlands, as Blar Breacan Phuill.

St Andrew and his companion travelled

many miles across the sea, standing on top of the stone until at length they reached land. The land they reached was in Portree in Skye, but the stone would not settle there and the root of the flower placed into the ground did not grow. St Andrew knew that this was not the place and he and his companion stepped back onto the stone.

The stone once again raised itself up and it sailed across the sea and this time came to Ireland. But the stone did not settle there, nor did the flower grow. St Andrew wanted to go back onto the stone but his companion said no and said he would stay on in Ireland. St Andrew travelled across the sea on the stone and came back to Skye.

This time he came to a place called Glendale, but the stone did not settle there. However, when St Andrew tried the root of the flower in the ground near a burn, it grew. St Andrew knew that this was a place where a huge Christian uprising would come from. But the stone had not settled, so St Andrew returned to the stone.

Once again the stone moved out into the sea and this time it headed down to Argyll.

At Argyll it came up over the land over the Moss of Dunad until it came to Dunad Hill, *Ard Dunad*. The stone lifted itself up to the very top of the hill, with St Andrew still upon it, and when it reached the top of the hill the stone settled down there and St Andrew knew this was the place where the Stone of Destiny should remain. He himself left the stone and made his way back to the Holy land, where later he was crucified on a saltire cross, which is commemorated in the flag of Scotland.

The stone remained at Dunad for many, many years and centuries. All the kings of Scotland were crowned on that stone at Dunad. Beside the stone were carvings the shape of a Boar and the footstep of a King. Some time later the kings of Scotland decided that Dunad was no longer the place to be crowned. The stone was moved to Scone, near Perth, and there the crowning ceremonies went on. Then the stone was moved to yet another place in Perth, and still the crowning ceremonies were held on the stone. People believed that if kings were not crowned upon this stone then they did not have the power of a king.

In 1297, Edward the First came into Scotland

with his troops, invaded Scotland, marched through it and took the Stone of Destiny, or Jacob's Pillow, from where it was kept near Perth to take it down to England. The stone was placed in the coronation throne, where the kings of England were crowned and later on the kings and queens of Britain. The stone remained there doing its purpose until very recently it came back to Scotland, where it rightfully belongs.

And the flower still grows wild in Glendale, which is the only place in Britain, perhaps in Europe, where the Blood Spot Flower grows wild.

The Farmer's Wife – *Bean Tuathanach*

THERE WAS A FARMER not all that far from here. He was a very good farmer. He worked his fields well and he had good cattle. He worked hard, very hard. He expanded his farm by acquiring more land when the time was right and worked the land well, so that his farm began to flourish and he was able to stock it up with good cattle. Eventually, he became the biggest farmer in the area. He was known for the best cattle, the best crops and he had lots of people working for him. He decided he would build himself a grand house. He had the house built and it was a beautiful big house. After a while he thought to himself, 'There is something missing. I have a beautiful house. I have top class cattle and first class crops, many people working for me. But there is something … there is something else I should have. I wonder what it is.'

He thought for a while about this until the poor silly man decided what he needed was a wife. Having decided he needed a wife he got on with the matter very quickly. Down in the village near to him there lived a very beautiful young girl. He thought that she would be just the wife for him. She was beautiful, hard working and she was a fine figure of a woman; good full breasts and fine wide childbearing hips. 'She would be just ideal,' he thought.

So off he went to see the girl's parents. He told the parents that he had decided he wanted to marry their daughter. The parents were quite taken by this idea because they thought that he was a big farmer who had plenty of money. He had all the things a man should have. He had a fine big house and plenty of folk working for him. He would do very well for their daughter. When the daughter came home, they told her that the farmer had come and wanted her for his wife.

But the daughter said, 'I am not too sure about that. He is a lot older than me and what about his vim and vigour that I would be expecting?'

'Ah', said the parents, 'That is a trivial kind of matter. The things you should be looking at are that he has got a fine big house, servants; everything a man should have he has got.

He has good cattle, good crops and he must have money put away somewhere. Now if you were to marry him, all that could be yours, because, as you said, he is quite a lot older than you and he might not last that long. A few years wouldn't matter really.'

The girl was still not happy about it, because she was thinking she would rather be bedded by a fine virile young man than an older man like this, but the parents persuaded her that he would be plenty and he would be good enough for her, and the girl gave in. The marriage was held and it was a fine great wedding. The couple went home and strange to say, it was a very happy marriage indeed. The farmer adored his young wife and she was good in the house. She did the cooking; all the things that should be done around the house, she did. At night their lovemaking was wonderful.

But then one day as the farmer was in the village, he saw people about and heard them talking. He came home and sat down to speak to his wife. 'These people were saying when they saw you, 'It's the farmer's wife and she is a beautiful woman'. They shouldn't be saying such things about my wife. You are my wife, you are mine and you belong to me. They shouldn't say things like that.' So he told his wife that she was not to go into the village again. The girl was one of these strange things, an obedient wife, and she did not go into the village again.

After a while the farmer started to think again, about his wife going out into the fields, and the people working in the fields seeing her and saying, 'She is the farmer's wife and she is a beautiful woman.' The farmer thought 'They shouldn't be saying such things about my wife. She is my wife.' He told the wife that she was to stay only in the garden and in the house, she was not to go outside into the fields anymore. And she did as she was told and happiness was still there.

Then one day the farmer watched his wife out in the garden doing bits here and there. He noticed that some of the servants were looking over the hedge and seeing his wife there. He said to himself, 'These people there, they are looking and saying, 'Oh, that's the farmer's wife. She is a beautiful woman.' They have no right to say that. She is my wife. She is mine!'

He told the wife she was not to go out into the garden. Again the wife obeyed him and stayed within the house and once again for a time happiness was theirs. But then one day the farmer thought to himself, 'There is my wife moving about inside the house. She will be passing the window. People will see her and the servants inside the house see her, and they will be saying, 'Oh, that's the farmer's wife and she is a beautiful woman.' They have no right to say that. She is my wife. Mine!'

He told the wife that she was to stay inside the house and he was going to board up all the windows, so that people outside could not possibly see anything. The wife again obeyed him, although she felt very sad about this.

Time moved on and happiness still was there. The farmer would come home at night, his wife would be waiting for him, and they would have their supper and then off to bed to enjoy their lovemaking. But once again the farmer started thinking and this time he thought to himself, 'Well, there is my wife inside the house and there are servants helping in the house. They are seeing her and they will be saying, 'That's the farmer's wife and she is a beautiful woman.' They have no right to say that. She is my wife. She is mine!' And the farmer locked his wife into the bedroom. He would not allow her out at all.

The wife stayed locked in the bedroom and when the farmer came home every night, he would open the door and go in and still happiness of a kind was there. But the wife was becoming sickly and ill. The farmer didn't notice. Then one night he came home and his wife was lying dead in the locked bedroom.

The farmer was broken hearted. Now too late he realised all the love and joy they had shared. He took the wife and gave her a great funeral but it didn't ease his grief at all. He went back to the house and now it was a lonely house, even though he had servants. He would realise over and over again how much he had lost through his own selfish fault. But he could do nothing about it.

After a year and a day the farmer was in the house one night when he heard a knock at the door. He went to the door and standing there was a little man with a white pointed beard and wide sparkling blue eyes. It was the brightest sparkle in someone's eyes the farmer had ever seen and this man was dressed all in brown. The man asked the farmer for hospitality and the farmer who, in his own way, was a good enough man invited the stranger in, fed him well and gave him a comfortable bed for the night, as was the custom for hospitality. In the morning he made sure that the little man got a good breakfast and then, as the little man was preparing to leave, he said to the farmer; 'Tell me, is there a wish you would have, one wish that you would truly like?'

The farmer looked at the little man and said, 'Oh, I have a wish, but no one can grant me my wish.'

The little man said to him, 'Well now, I don't know about that but tell me what your wish is and I'll see what can be done about it.'

'Ah', said the farmer. 'The wish that I would wish is that I would have my dear lovely wife back again.'

'Oh', said the little man, 'But it was yourself who killed her.'

'I know that.' said the farmer. 'And I have never ever forgotten it in this year and a day. I have wept often for her and wish her back. I wish I had never been so bad as to do the things I did to her but in any case, no one can grant my wish.' The little man went off. The farmer went to his work as usual around the different fields and came back at night to the house. When he walked into the house, who was there to greet him but his beautiful wife, restored again to all her former beauty. The farmer was delighted. Now happiness again was theirs.

Their life together was wonderful; their lovemaking was even more passionate. Everything was magical. But then again the farmer started to think and he thought, 'Those people in the village are looking and saying, 'Oh, that is the farmer's beautiful wife.'
They have no right to say that. She is my wife,' and he forbade his wife to go into the village.

She obeyed him. And then again the farmer forbade her to go out of the garden. Once again she obeyed him. Then he forbade her to go out of the house. She obeyed him and he boarded up the windows as before. And then came the time when he forbade her to leave the bedroom, locked the door so she could not get out and went away to work in his fields as usual.

When he came back that night he walked up the stairs, unlocked the bedroom door and stepped inside. And there in the bed was the shape of his beautiful, wonderful, obeying wife lying under the bed covers. 'Oh, the darling,' the farmer thought, 'She is lying there ready, waiting for me. She is so wonderful.' He got hold of the blankets and pulled them off the bed so that he could see his darling beautiful wife. But when he did so he started back in horror, for lying on the bed in the shape of his beautiful wife was this thing, a thing composed of bones, and in between the bones there were yellow maggots and white maggots and green slimy puss. As he looked, the thing raised its hands towards him. As its arms lifted, he could see the green puss dripping from the ends of the fingers, which now were just bony points. The thing said to him, 'Come to me, my darling. Come into my arms.' The farmer turned to run back out of the door, but the door was gone. He looked for the window to jump, but the window was gone. He looked around himself realising that he was enclosed in a great cavern, like a tomb. He looked back and there was the thing tottering towards him with its arms out saying, 'Come into my arms, my beloved. Come to my arms.'

The farmer realised that because of what he had done to his wife he was condemned to stay forever in this cavern with this thing that had once been his beautiful wife. When the realisation came to him he screamed and he screamed and he screamed.

The Girl from under the Sea – *Cala Lochlanaich*

A CROFTER AND HIS WIFE lived in a small house on their croft beside the sea. In their lives they had much happiness along with hard toil and some sadness, as was the way of the world. The crofter had a small boat and would often go out on the sea to help their store of food for the winter. Yet even in this there was danger for it was known that, apart from the usual changes of wind and waves, that area of the sea was a favourite place for the people from under the sea. They were cruel heartless people and would capsize a small boat just for fun to then watch and laugh as the fisherman drowned. They were spoken of in whispers and by various names such as *Lochlanaich*, the people from under the sea; *Duine Gorm*, the blue men; *Saighe Mhara*, sea bitches, and other even less complimentary terms. So the people from the sea were feared and hated by the people of the land. No mercy was given to anyone who had a good word for or tried to help the people from the sea.

Now the crofter and his wife had one great regret in their life and this was that they had no family. The wife was now approaching an age when any chance of having a child was very remote. One day the crofter and his wife were down beside the sea, gathering seaweed to fertilize their croft. As they raked and forked the seaweed into heaps they saw an elderly woman approaching them. As she came near to them she slipped and fell heavily on the slippery rocks. The crofter and his wife ran to help her. She told them she was not hurt just shaken and asked if they had a drink of water. They gave her water and started to talk to her, although they did not recognize her. As they spoke, she said to them, 'I see you have no children and this makes your hearts heavy.'

'Indeed that is true,' they admitted, 'but we are used to it now and although we would dearly love a child of our own, we accept we will never have one.'

'Don't give up hope,' said the old woman. 'If I can promise you will have a child, would you also take care of a child from the sea?'

At that they looked more closely at the old woman and realised that she was one of the people from under the sea, and fear came upon them. But she said not to be afraid for if they really wanted a child and would take care of the sea baby, no harm would come to them and happiness would be theirs.

For the thought of having their own child they agreed to the bargain, although the old woman warned them that they must be prepared to allow the child from the sea to leave them whenever it reached an age at which it wished to leave, and they should put no obstacles in its path. The bargain was sealed and the old woman walked into the sea and disappeared.

The crofter and his wife went home. They told no one of their bargain or of the old woman, but within weeks the wife discovered she was pregnant. The child was born, a fine healthy boy, and they were delighted, but when the baby was only a few days old, and its mother full of milk, they were down by the sea when they heard the cry of a baby and found it laying behind the rock, a baby girl. The baby was very beautiful and they were full of pity for it lying there cold, naked and hungry. The wife picked it up and snuggled it close to her and fed it, and the realisation came on them that this was the baby from the sea they had promised to take care of. The crofter and his wife were honest and warm-hearted people and they reared the sea baby with their own. And if people questioned them, they said it was a foster child from relations who lived far away. As the custom of fostering was a great tradition in the Highlands, this was readily accepted.

As time went on the couple came to look on the children as if both were their own. Each was loved as much as the other and there was no difference in the way they were treated. One difference between the children was that while the boy treated the sea with a mixture of fear and respect, the girl loved the sea and was noted for her swimming prowess and her fearlessness when in a boat. In fact some compared her to the sea people and said she could even swim as well as them. The children knew they were foster brother and sister but their love for each other was even greater than that between siblings. For as a Gaelic proverb has it: 'Though great is the love between brothers, yet seven times greater is that between fosters.'

So the years went happily by until the girl was about twelve years of age, when a restlessness came upon her and she wanted to leave her home. Forgetful of their promise, the crofter and his wife tried to persuade her to stay, even locking her into her room, but despite all their attempts there came a day when she ran down the croft and plunged into the sea and was seen no more. Her foster brother was broken hearted at the loss of her for, unbeknown to their parents, they pledged themselves to each other and promised eternal love. Now she was gone and for him the joy had left the world.

Time moved on as it always does. The boy grew to a man and became a good seaman and skipper of his own fishing boat. Yet despite being a fine looking man and much liked by the girls, he gave himself to none in love. One day his fishing boat was caught in a fierce storm and despite all their efforts she began to sink. As the ship foundered under him, he and his crew were flung into the sea. Their heavy boots and clothing dragged them down into the deep green depths and one by one they drowned. But as the skipper felt his life slipping from him, he felt a hand on his arm and saw in front of him his beloved foster sister. She pressed her lips to his, breathed her breath into his lungs and told him she had been true to him as he had been to her. Then she led him down to a place below the sea where stood a fine city built of white marble, within the centre a great palace.

She took him into the palace and with great joy told her family, the king and queen of Lochlann, that this was the one for whom she had waited so long and who had had her heart since they were children together. 'He and his parents gave me my life whereas all others would have taken it. Now I have given him his life and we will live together till all things change and our children are of both sea and land.'

So it was done. The link was made between the people from under the sea and those of the land, for love can alter all things and all people and the love of a woman can outlast the sun.

the old man of skye – *Bodach Sgith*

THERE WAS AN OLD MAN on the Isle of Skye. He had been there all of his life. He had never left the island and he was quite happy and content to stay there, but one day he was sitting beside the fire and he thought to himself, 'Well now, age is coming upon me and I have never seen anything but Skye. I wonder if I should maybe have a look at some other things. But what could I do?'

So he thought about it, and on the very next morning he thought to himself, 'Well, I have never seen the big cities, so I am going to go to see a big city.'

He got the boat and bus to Inverness and when he got to Inverness he was amazed by seeing all these people walking back and forth in the streets. Then there were the buses going up and down and the trains in the train station. He had never seen a train before in his life, and there were cars everywhere.

'Oh', he says, 'What an amazing place the big city is. I wonder what I should do while I am here.'

And he thought to himself, 'I know. I have never been in a supermarket. I have heard about them but I have never been in one before in my life.' So off he went up to Inches in Inverness to the supermarket. As he walked into the first one he looked and there were these great long aisles full of goods stretching into the distance and he looked and said, 'Oh, what a great big place this is. What a marvellous place the big city is.'

He started to walk down one of the aisles. As he walked down he looked at the tins that were piled on the shelves and as he looked he saw 'Ah, potato powder – add water and you have potato.'

'Oh my!' he said. 'What a wonderful place the big city is. If I had known about this when I was home in Skye, the work that I could have saved myself. There was I ploughing the field, planting the potatoes, weeding the potatoes, forking out the potatoes, putting them into a bag, carrying them in the bag up into my house, putting them into a clamp for the winter and then taking them out of the clamp to skin them and cook them. I could have saved myself all that work if I had only known about this. What a wonderful place the big city is.'

He moved on to the next stack in the aisle and there it was, 'Powdered egg – add water and you have egg.' The old man of Skye stood back in amazement again. 'Oh my! What a place the big city is! If I had known about this when I was home in Skye, the amount of work it would have saved me. To think there was I feeding those hens, giving them the very best so I could get eggs from them. Here I was cleaning out their hen house, cutting hay to pad their hen house, carrying up the eggs and then cooking the eggs all the different ways, boiling them or frying them. Oh, what a wonderful place the big city is. If I had known about this, all the work it would have saved me.' And he moved on to the next pile of cans.

The next pile of cans was 'Powdered Milk – add water and you have milk'. 'Oh my!' the old man of Skye said. 'If I had known about this when I was home in Skye, the work it would have saved me. What a wonderful place the big city is! When I think on it, there I had these cows and I milked them and I carried the milk up to the house, I skimmed the milk and used it. I had to cut hay and corn to feed the cows. I had to muck out their byre and put fresh hay in so they wouldn't be standing on the cold floor of the byre. To think of all the work I put in. What a wonderful place the big city is!'

He moved on to the next stack of tins. He looked and there it was – 'Baby Powder'. He looked in astonishment and stepped back and said, 'Oh no! No, the old ways are the best. I am away back home to Skye.'

This story was written by myself about 30 years ago, after taking a young person who had never been off Skye to Inverness and observing their reactions to the big city.

the silver chanter

HE MACCRUIMENS WERE the greatest piping family who ever lived. Their Piobearachds are still played to this very day. None have ever surpassed them. One of the greatest of the MacCruimen pipers was well known because on his pipes he had a silver chanter.

A number of years ago there was a MacCruimen piper who was a great piper but he always wanted to be better and better. No matter how good he got, he felt he could be better still. One day he was up on the hill practising with his pipes as usual when he heard a noise behind him. He turned and looked and there was a small little man behind him. The little man said to him, 'Patrick MacCruimen you are indeed a master piper. We have a wedding on and we have no one to pipe at it. Would you come with me and pipe for us? You would be doing us a great service if you would do this.' This man was one of the little people – *An Duine Shithean*, the fairies.

Patrick MacCruimen said to the little man, 'I will come with you but I will only play for the one night for the wedding and then I must come back to my own people.' The little man promised him that this would be so. He led Patrick MacCruimen Oig down the hill to where a great big door stood open at the hill and Patrick Oig, although he did trust the little man, also remembered what he had been told and as he entered the great door he slipped a penny from his sporran into the hinge of the door, so that he would be able to get out again when the time came. The little man took Patrick Oig inside the hill. There was a huge hall all decorated for the wedding and there was the bride and the groom and all the others connected with the ceremony. The little man said to Patrick Oig, 'Now play for us.' Patrick Oig filled his pipes and played. He played for the ceremony and he played for the dance after. He played and he played. He felt he had never played in this way before. The little people were delighted and they danced the whole night away. Merriment and happiness was theirs, and his too. And so it went on and then they heard the cock crowing outside, heralding the coming of the dawn. Patrick Oig said, 'Now I must leave you.' The little man walked to the great door with him. Patrick Oig pushed the door open and stepped outside and the little man stepped outside with him.

The little man said to Patrick Oig, 'You are indeed a master piper but I will give you something now that will make you the greatest piper of all time.' And he handed to Patrick Oig a silver chanter. He said to Patrick Oig, 'As long as you have that in your pipes there will not be in this entire world anyone who could surpass you in playing. But you must always remember that you must never ever curse your chanter in any way or you will lose it and your skill of the pipes. This is a gift for you because you gave your gift to us and we must give you something in return.' Patrick Oig thanked the little man, fitted the silver chanter to his pipes and made his way back to Borreraig.

Now when Patrick Oig played the pipes, people came from all around, from miles around to listen, and others came to learn. And Patrick Oig for years was the greatest piper that ever the world had known and perhaps is to this very day.

But one day Patrick Oig was coming in a boat from Dunvegan Castle and in the boat was the chief of MacLeod, whom the MacCruimens always piped for. Patrick Oig was playing his pipes standing on the bow of the boat proud as could be and his pipes rang out over the loch. But the loch was a bit rough that day and the spray was dashing up from the bow of the boat and hitting Patrick Oig. He was not caring about that in the least but then the spray covered the silver chanter. It became slippery and Patrick Oig's fingers started to slide on the chanter, making the occasional note that was not just right. Patrick Oig in a fit of temper cursed the chanter and said to it, 'Can you not stop being sloppy, you clown of a chanter! You are no use to me like that.' When he said that, the chanter pulled itself clear of the pipes, plunged into the water and was gone.

When Patrick Oig landed back in Borreraig his skill in his fingers too was gone and he was no longer the greatest piper in the entire world.

annag maccruimen

THE MacCRUIMENS WERE great pipers and they did not believe that women should be discriminated against doing piping. If a woman was as good a piper as a man then she was credited with that and hailed as a great piper. One of these was Anna MacCruimen. She was a great piper, as good as any man, and she played for the MacCruimens. At this time the MacCruimens every year held a contest at their school of piping in Borreraig and anyone from anywhere could play against them. At the end of the evening the pipers would decide who had been the greatest piper, but always a MacCruimen won. For the MacCruimens had a way of fingering that was different to any other pipers and this way of fingering they would teach to none.

One of the great pipers of that time in Glendale was a man with the name of Hugh Macpherson and every year he would go and compete at the College of Piping. But although he was a great piper, still the MacCruimens were better. Hugh Macpherson and Anna MacCruimen fell in love. They went out with each other, wandered the hills together and the following year, when the piping contest was held again at Borreraig, Hugh Macpherson was the last of the pipers to play. When he stepped up to play in front of the sounding wall, everyone there realised he was the greatest piper of all of them. For not only had he his own great skill of piping, but he had acquired the MacCruimens fingering.

The MacCruimens had to admit he was the best on the day but they were furious about this, for they knew that someone must have broken the family tradition and taught him the MacCruimen fingering. Only one person could have done that and that was Anna MacCruimen. After the piping was over and the pipers had dispersed to their different places, Anna MacCruimen was called in front of the MacCruimen council. She told them yes she had taught Hugh Macpherson the MacCruimen fingering. For the love of him she had taught him this. The MacCruimen's were furious at this and they said that, to make sure she never taught the fingering to anyone else, her hand would be laid on a block and all her fingers of her right hand would be chopped off. This was carried out there and then and Anna MacCruimen was deprived of her fingers on her right hand. But Hugh Macpherson stood by her and they married and moved to Glendale. There they had a big family, several of them pipers, but when Anna MacCruimen heard what would be done to her she put a curse on the MacCruimens. She said that, 'The day would come and not long distant when the greatest of the MacCruimen pipers would be killed in battle. And there would be none, not one single MacCruimen, from that time fit to pipe in the hall of MacLeod. Then a Macpherson of Glendale would become a piper to MacLeod.' This was the year 1739.

After she had gone and lived with Hugh Macpherson, there came the 1745 uprising and in it the last of the great MacCruimen pipers was killed in the battle of Moy, and there was none fit to pipe in the hall of MacLeod. A Macpherson of Glendale then became the piper for a time to MacLeod of MacLeod, but it is noted of the branch of Macphersons of which Anna MacCruimen was the progenitor, that in every generation of the family there is at least one piper and at least one was left handed. This pertains even to the present day, as I can show for myself.

This was a very old traditional family story, which was passed on within the family and kept within the family always.

one of those who search always

THERE WAS A YOUNG LAD in Ardnamurchan in a little village called Shielfoot. This young lad always wanted to find something different, to make his mark in the world; perhaps with wealth or perhaps as a great artist of some kind, or a great musician. Whatever it was, he really wanted to do it. One day he was down at the side of the shore and at the side of the shore he saw strange boat; just a small boat. He looked at it and he said, 'This doesn't belong to anybody around here. I wonder whose boat that is.'

He climbed into the boat just to see who it belonged to or where it came from. As he climbed into it, the boat suddenly spun around and headed off across the sea. The boat went so fast the boy was terrified; he clung to its sides as best as he could. Although they went against the wind and the tide, the boat still headed on at great speed. They reached a bank of mist and, plunged into it, the boy could not see anything. He looked; he tried to listen as he couldn't see anything because of the mist, but still there was nothing. But he could feel the movement of the boat under him. Then all of a sudden the mist lifted and he saw in front of him a beautiful green island which he had never seen before.

The boat grounded on the beach of the green island and the boy went ashore. When he went ashore he was greeted by a beautiful tall woman who took him up to her house and fed him well. Then she said to him, 'You are one of those who search always.'

The boy said, 'Yes, that is true indeed. I have always looked for something but I am not sure what I look for.'

'Well', said the woman, 'Stay with us for a short time and perhaps you'll find what you are looking for.'

The boy stayed on the island for a time and he tried music, but it was not really for him. He tried many different things, different crafts; wood-turning, wood-carving, but they were not for him. Then one day he came upon an old man sitting by himself and the old man was painting characters in a book. The boy looked and watched the man and immediately he felt this was what he wanted to do. He sat beside the old man and learned from him, and it seemed after a few days he suddenly no longer wanted to stay on the island. He wanted to leave the island again.

On that day, with the sun shining brightly, he made his way down to the shore to take a boat to try to get back home, wherever home was. The tall woman came up to him on the shore and said to him, 'You have chosen your gift. Use it wisely.' A boat appeared on the sea and the woman helped the boy into the boat, then the boat took off. Once again it came into a great bank of mist and the boy did not know how or where he was going. The boat carried on through the mist and came out the other side and there, straight ahead of the boy, was the coast of Ardnamurchan; a part he knew, below the waterfall at Shielfoot.

He stepped out of the boat and it immediately turned and sailed away. The boy went up to the village of Shielfoot and he was met there by many, who said to him, 'But how have you come back now?' The boy looked at them and they were people he had known when he was at school and playing in the hills, but now they were old. They looked at him and said, 'You look the same age you where when you disappeared. How can this be? You have been away for 21 years.'

The boy was amazed, but he got himself some parchment and pens, brushes and colours. Then he started to paint these signs. He made a whole book of signs with different colours and different symbols. When the book was full he closed the book and looked around him. No one was left alive of the ones he had known in his youth. The boy took the book and hid it carefully where it would be kept safe and dry, then he went down to the shore. The boat came again and the boy stepped into the boat, knowing that he would never ever come back to the land of Ardnamurchan for he was going now to the other world. And this time he would not return.

This story was told to me by my grand uncle John Cameron of Shielfoot, about 1942–43, during the war. I have heard versions of it since then.

Sgiath's Gift to Love – *Tiodhlaic Sgiath an Gaol*

WORD CAME THAT the Northern Men – the *Lochlannaich*, the people from under the sea – had gathered together a huge fleet of galleys and were going to raid into Skye. Sgiath, the great queen of Skye at this time, decided that what she must do was meet them on the water, fight them at sea and break them. She gathered together all the galleys and birlinns she could and she and her amazon warriors went to meet the Vikings. They met in the Minch and there was a terrible fight, a great sea battle, and at the end of the battle Sgiath's forces prevailed and the Vikings fled, those that could. Of the rest only two were captured. They were brought to Skye to the stronghold of Sgiath and brought before Sgiath herself. As she looked she said to them, 'Why have you fought against me? What are your names?'

The first one said that he was Hagar, Hagar the Slaughterer. With his great axe he had killed many men and everyone quailed before him.

Sgiath said to him, 'We did not quail before you, neither I nor my amazons. Now you are conquered.'

She said to the other one, 'And who are you?'

He looked at Sgiath and he said, 'I, I am Conran the Harper. When I play the harp everyone stops to listen, even the birds stop singing the better to hear. I can play men into a trance and my music is magical.'

Sgiath said to him, 'Why then did you fight against me?'

Conran said, 'I fight always to find death. But I have never found it yet.'

Sgiath looked at the pair of them and said to them, 'Tell me, have you known love?'

Hagar laughed and said, 'Of course I have known love. I have loved hundreds of women and no one has ever gone away unsatisfied from my loving.'

Sgiath looked at him and said, 'You have never known love.'

She said to her amazon warriors, 'Take him away and use him as a slave in the kitchens and other places.'

She looked at Conran and said, 'Have you ever known love?'

Conran replied, 'Oh yes, I have known love and that is why I now seek death. Years ago, when I was a young man, I loved and she loved me too. Our love was great and our happiness was great. But then one night, as we slept in an encampment, noises woke us up and we went out to see, to hear that raiders had come upon us. They were killing men, women and children. I took my sword to kill them too but even as I did so my beloved came out behind me and took through her body the spear that was meant to be in my back. She fell there, dead. I went into a wild red fury and I fought and killed and slew until the raiders fled. But my beloved was dead and I was dead too. I was dead in spirit. Since then I have sought always to die myself, as I then could join my beloved. I have fought anyone who would take me. I have fought everywhere I could. But still death did not come.'

Sgiath looked at him and said, 'Truly you have known love. I too have known love. The love I had was for one man only and he is gone. There will be none else. Play for us the clarsach, the harp. Let us hear what magic you have in the harp.'

Conran picked up the harp and he played.

As he played, it was as if a trance came on all in that place, as though they were under a spell. Conran played; the birds stopped singing, as he said they would, and gathered around to listen. Such music has never been heard before or since. Conran played on and it was as though a great sleep came on every person in that place and Conran played on. When he stopped, all awoke in an instant.

Sgiath said to Conran, 'Surely and truly you have known love and grief and sorrow and misery.' She said to her amazons, 'This man deserves to find his peace, to remove his misery.'

Sgiath and her amazons took Conran down to the shore and there they staked him out between four stakes, naked. They lit a fire near to him and as the fire burned down the red embers were there. Sgiath herself took the bright red embers and laid them on the chest of Conran until his heart started to swell and swell until it burst. At last Conran died.

Sgiath said, 'Surely this man knew love and gave love and his love will last forever.'

the cup of healing – *cupan beatha*

IT HAD BEEN A LONG hard day of hunting in the Cuillins. One of those days in Skye when the mist was heavy and wet and it soaked you right through your skin. Fionn and the other Fianna had been hunting all day and now were heading back tired, wet and dreary. When they reached the place they were camping, the covers had been put up, the fires were lit and they had food to eat and wine and other things to drink. They made merry and then, as the night came down heavier, they retired under the covers.

As Fionn was lying there, he heard this scratching noise near his cover. He lifted the edge of the cover and looked and there was the ugliest woman he had ever seen in his life. She was old, wrinkled and twisted. Her face was covered with warts and pustules. Her nose ended in a great hook and her chin came up to meet it. And she said to Fionn, 'Please let me under the cover. I want to get out of this terrible wind and rain. Just let me into a corner.'

Fionn just looked at her and said, 'You ugly

old hag, I would not let you under the covers even if you were my mother. Get away from me.' And the old woman sadly went away.

She came to the cover of Ossian. He was sleeping soundly, wrapped in his plaid beneath the cover. When he heard the scratching on his cover he looked and there was this ugly old hag of a woman. The ugliest woman he had ever seen in all his born days. She said to him, 'Please let me come under the covers, just into a corner out of this terrible weather.'

Ossian looked at her and said, 'No, you are the ugliest, most horrible looking woman I have ever seen in my life. I will not let you under the covers even into a corner. Get away from me.' The old hag looked even sadder and moved away. Ossian put down the edge of the cover again.

Caoilte was lying sleeping soundly, dreaming of the hunt in the hills, when he heard this scratching on his cover. The scratching went on and on until he could no longer disregard it. He went across and lifted the corner of the cover and there was this hag. The most dreadful looking woman he had ever seen in his life. Wrinkled and twisted; horrible to look upon.

Her face covered with warts and pustules. Caoilte looked at her and said, 'What do you want?'

The woman said, 'Please let me in, just under a corner of the cover, so that I can be dry for this one night. Please let me in?'

Caoilte looked at her and said, 'No. No, I will not let you anywhere near me. You are the most horrible looking hag I have ever seen in my life. I would not have you even in the least corner of my cover. Get away from me and don't come back again' He put down the corner of the cover and the old hag sadly went on her way.

She came to the cover of Diarmaid and she scratched on the cover and Diarmaid woke. He looked out and saw the old hag there. She said to him, 'Please let me come under a corner of your cover. Just let me get warm there, let me be dry out of this terrible weather.' And Diarmaid was not only the bravest and the most handsome of all the Fianna, he was also the most tender hearted. He looked at her and said, 'You are the most horrible looking hag I have ever seen in my life but you shall have a corner of the cover. I would turn no one away on a night such as this.' And he allowed the old woman to come in and go into a corner of the cover. The old woman settled into a corner and Diarmaid wrapped himself back into his plaid and lay there comfortably. After a little while he heard the old woman saying, 'Oh Diarmaid, Diarmaid, please let me under your plaid. Just a little bit to give me some warmth. I am so cold here because I was soaked outside. I am so cold. Just give me a corner of your plaid to keep me warm.'

Diarmaid looked at her and once again he said, 'You are the most horrible looking hag I have ever seen in my life but I can see you are cold and shivering and wet. I will let you come under the plaid with me but try not to come against me. I would not like the feel of you against me at all.' The old woman lifted part of the plaid and slipped under beside Diarmaid, and as soon as she slipped under the plaid, she turned into the most beautiful woman that Diarmaid had ever seen in all his life. And so the two of them had a wonderful night together, both wrapped into the plaid of Diarmaid.

In the morning Diarmaid got up, folded his plaid into his phillimore, put it on and went out, and with him walked the beautiful woman he had slept with the night before. The first person he met was Fionn. Fionn looked and said to the woman, 'You are the most beautiful looking woman I have ever seen in my life. Oh, if you were to come to me I would shelter and help you.' The woman looked at him and said to him, 'Fionn, you had your chance last night and you cast me out.'

As they continued on they met Ossian. Ossian looked at the woman and he said to her, 'Ah, you are the most beautiful looking woman I have ever seen in all my life. If you were to stay with me, all the poetry I would write for you, the most beautiful poems you ever heard in your life; wonderful poems of the hunt and love I would write for you.'

'Ha!' said the woman. 'Ossian, you had your chance last night and you threw me out.'

They continued on and met Caoilte. Caoilte looked at the woman and he said, 'You are the most beautiful, the most wonderfully formed woman I have ever seen in all my born days. If you were mine I would hunt the hill for you. I would outrun the deer and bring them to you so you would never want.'

'Ha!', said the woman. 'You had your chance last night, Caoilte and you threw me out.' And they carried on.

Diamaid and the woman passed out of the camp followed by a great bitch, Diarmaid's hunting dog. This great bitch was heavy with pups. The woman said to Diarmaid, 'Diarmaid, what would you like most in this world?'

Diarmaid said, 'Well, I would love to have a fine castle down near the shore, and in the castle I could live happily with you. For as long as we would both be together we could be happy. But also with my dog and its pups.'

The woman said, 'Is that the wish of your heart, Diarmaid?'

'It is indeed.' said Diarmaid.

'Well,' said the woman. 'I could give you your wish, but you must remember that you must never cast up to me of how I was when you first saw me.'

Diarmaid promised he would never cast this up to her and would always be faithful and true to her.

They camped out for the night on the hill and in the morning, when they woke up, down there above the shore was a huge fine castle.

They walked into the castle and Diarmaid's faithful hound followed him in. In the castle was everything he could wish for, all the very best of furnishings, and Diarmaid and the woman settled down there and lived very happily together.

Diarmaid said to the woman, 'There is one thing you must never do. You must never give away any of my dogs.'

Diarmaid went out hunting again and the bitch had two pups. Diarmaid left the two pups in the care of the woman, and as he went out he said, 'Remember, you must never give away any of my dogs.'

The woman stayed in the castle with the dogs when a man came to the door and asked for hospitality. As was the custom, hospitality was given. He came in, was fed and given a bed for the night. In the morning the woman said to him, 'What gift will you have from the house?' For it was a custom that a guest leaving the house would always be given a gift, and the gift would be what he or she asked for.

The man looked at her and he said, 'There is just one gift I would like. Give me one of the pups.'

The woman said, 'I can't give you that. These are the pups from my husband's bitch and he would not be very pleased at all if I gave you one.'

The man said, 'Would you break the custom of years? I am sure your husband would be very insulted if you broke the great tradition'

The woman thought, 'Well, if I give him one pup we still have the other pup and the bitch. Surely Diarmaid can stand with that, and she gave the man one of the pups.'

When Diarmaid came back from the hill and discovered that one of the pups was gone he said to the woman, 'What have you done with my pup?'

The woman said to him, 'A stranger came here and got hospitality, and in the morning he asked for a pup as his gift.'

Diarmaid said, 'You silly fool. You clown of a woman. What do you think of giving him one of my pups? I told you, you are never to give away any of my dogs. And to think that you, who were nothing but an ugly old hag when I first saw you, should do a thing like that to me.'

The woman said, 'That is the first time.'

Life went on with them. They were living happily there and Diarmaid again went to the hill with the bitch. The woman was in the castle by herself and there came a stranger to the door who asked for hospitality. He was granted hospitality and in the morning, on leaving, he was asked what gift he would have.

He said, 'The gift I would have is that pup. She is a nice little pup.'

The woman said, 'No, that gift I can not give. That is my husband's.'

The stranger said, 'You would break the laws of hospitality? You would insult this house? Insult your husband by refusing me the gift I asked for?'

Once again the woman thought, 'Diarmaid himself would not break the law of hospitality of the house. He would not give up the great tradition,' and again she gave the pup to the man.

When Diarmaid came back from the hill he was even more angered. 'What have you done with my pup?' he said.

The women told him that a stranger had come and demanded the pup as a gift.

Diarmaid said to her, 'I told you, you are never to give away any of my dogs. You, you would do this to me, and I was so kind to you when you were nothing but a dirty, wet, sniffling old hag. I took you in.'

The woman said, 'That is the second time.'

A few days later Diarmaid was away with some of the other Fianna. He'd left the bitch at home in the castle with the woman, when an old woman came to the door and asked for hospitality. The woman took the old woman in and gave her hospitality of the best she had. The next morning, as the old woman was leaving the woman asked, 'What gift will you have?'

The old woman looked at her and said, 'The gift I would have is that bitch, the brindle bitch of Diarmaid.'

Diarmaid's woman looked at the old woman. 'No, I cannot give you that gift as it is my husband's most prized dog. She is everything to him.'

The old woman looked at her and said, 'You would stop me having the bitch and yet your husband himself would not stop me having it. He maintains all the great traditions. He is the most hospitable man who ever walked this earth and you would have me believe he would not grant the gift of hospitality?'

Once again the woman thought, 'Well, this is true enough of Diarmaid,' and she gave the old woman the bitch.

When Diarmaid came back he went into the castle and he immediately said, 'Where is my bitch? What have you done with her?'

The woman told him how the old woman had come and asked for the bitch as a gift. Diarmaid was furious. He said to her, 'You clown, you fool! What have you done? You have given away my bitch. The best dog ever I had. You, you would do this to me? You, whom I took in when no one else would take you in, when you were such an ugly hag of a woman that no one wanted to let you touch them and only I let you join me in my plaid.'

The woman said, 'That is the third and the last time.'

Diarmaid and the woman went back to bed that night but in the morning when Diarmaid woke up the woman had gone and so had his castle. All that was left of it was a mark in the ground of where it had been. Diarmaid was broken hearted now for he dearly loved the woman. He decided he would follow her tracks to wherever they would lead him.

He went on and the tracks led far away. They went across and then down, towards the sea at a different place.

As he went, he found a gout of blood at the side of the track. He picked it up and put it in his dorlainn, the leather satchel which was carried at the belt. And he carried on. Then he found a second gout of blood. He picked it up and put it into the dorlainn. Then he reached the sea, and there at the side of the sea was a third gout of blood. Diarmaid picked it up and put it into his dorlainn and carried on into the sea.

As he moved into the sea, the sea opened in front of him as if it was a tunnel going down below the sea. Diarmaid walked down the tunnel. He carried on walking down the tunnel until he came to a place, a great city below the sea, all built of shining white marble with people in the streets, everyone looking happy. Diarmaid carried on until he came to the greatest building in the place. When he arrived at the greatest building, the doors were flung open and he went inside.

Inside, the king of the Under-Sea-Land said to him, 'What have you done to my daughter?' Then the king led Diarmaid to a bedchamber and there lay the beautiful woman dying. Diarmaid was broken hearted now and said to the king. 'How can I save her? If there is anything I can do to save her, I will do it.'

The king said, 'There is only one way you can save her. You must go and get the cup of healing. It is the cup that heals all ill. You must go and get it and bring it back here. I will then fill it with water and you must crush into the cup the three gouts of blood and let the woman drink it. When she does this, all her love for you will turn into hate and you will never see her again.'

Diarmaid said, 'I am the one who has wronged her and I love her so much that I will do even this, although I will lose her.'

The king then told Diarmaid that to get the cup of healing he must go to another island and there he will meet dangers and adventures. On that island, right in the centre, he will find the cup of healing on an altar of the druids, but the cup is protected by a great serpent. Diamaid would have to overcome the great serpent to get the cup of healing.

Diarmaid bade farewell and went on his way. Once again he walked under the sea in what seemed like a tunnel of water until he came to the island of Hrumm. And on the island of Hrumm, as he walked across the island he saw a river, and sitting beside it was a little man all dressed in brown. Diarmaid looked at the river and saw it was a rough, fast flowing river. He knew that he would get thoroughly wet and perhaps carried away trying to cross it. The little man looked at Diarmaid and said, 'I see you are not very keen on crossing the water.'

'Well', said Diamaid, 'I want to cross it right enough but I don't want to get myself and my equipment soaking if I can avoid it.'

'Well, you can avoid it.' said the little man. 'I'll carry you across.'

Diarmaid looked at the little man and said, 'You are a quarter of the size of me. You could never carry me. Especially across a river as fierce as that!'

'Oh, I could.' said the little man. 'But if I do it you must make me a promise.'

'What is the promise?' said Diarmaid.

'When you come back with the cup', said the little man. 'You must allow me to drink from it.'

'Well,' said Diarmaid. 'I am sure that can be arranged. I can promise that.'

And with that the little man picked Diarmaid up on his shoulders. Then he ran across the surface of the water and put Diarmaid down at the far shore.

The little man said, 'There you are now. Carry on your way but remember your promise.'

Diarmaid carried on his way. He walked on for some miles until he came to the great square altar of the druids and on top of the altar, curled all round, was a serpent. Diamaid had never known or seen a serpent this huge in all his life. The serpent was wide awake. His tongue forked in and out and his eyes watched Diarmaid. Behind the snake, standing in the centre of the altar, was the cup of healing, but all around the cup were the coils of the serpent. Diarmaid looked and thought, 'Now if I take my sword and try to cut the head of the serpent, I am not sure I could cut it off with one blow because of the sheer size of it. Now how am I going to get to that cup?'

Then he thought of the woman lying there and the state she was in and at that his heart swelled, his courage came back to him and he made the great leap of the heroes and landed in the coils of the serpent. He picked up the cup and with the same leap carried it out of the coils, over the serpent's head and landed safely.

He tucked the cup into his dorlainn and started to walk back across the island, but this time he walked a different route so that he would not meet up with the little brown man. For he knew that this little man was one of the fairy people and if he gave the little man a drink from the cup, he would lose the cup and never see it again. He took a different route around, up over the hills and down again to the sea where he had first come out. Once again, when he walked into the sea it was as though a tunnel came around him, a tunnel made of water. He walked through the tunnel, down deep into the sea, until he came again to the great white city. When he arrived at the great white city he walked into the shiny palace of the king and said to him, 'I have the cup.'

The king said, 'I will fill it with water and you must crush the gouts of blood into the water.'

The king filled the cup with water and Diarmaid crushed the gouts of blood into the cup and stirred them in well. Then he went to the chamber where the woman was lying. Diarmaid looked at her. She looked so beautiful lying there, in spite of her illness, that he thought, 'If I give her a drink from the cup she will hate me and I will never see her again. Can I stand that? Would it not be better not to let her drink and I might perhaps have some little time of happiness left with her?'

But then he thought to himself, 'No. This is my fault. I am to blame for all this. If I had not acted as I did, she would still be with me.'

He bent forward and propped her up in the bed, and gave her a drink from the cup. The moment she drank from the cup she became well again and she looked at Diarmaid and said to him. 'You, you are nothing to me now. Go from me. I never want to see you again.'

Diarmaid turned and walked out of the chamber, saddened and distressed. When he walked out of the chamber the king was there and he said to him, 'I told you, Diarmaid, that if you gave her a drink from the cup she would hate you and you would never see her again. But you have done your very best for my daughter. You have done what a good man should and so I will give you something, Diarmaid, that will make up for losing her. It is a gift for you.'

The king put his finger into the centre of the forehead of Diarmaid. When he took the finger away there was as if a burn had been made in the centre of Diarmaid's forehead. 'Now,' said the king. 'From now on, any woman who sees that mark upon you will immediately fall in love with you, regardless of whom they are, high or low. You can go back to your own land now.'

Diarmaid walked down the tunnel again and came out of the water at the shore where he had first started. He looked around thinking, 'Things have changed somehow.' But he went on, when he came upon the camp of the Fianna. In the camp of Fionn he was welcomed very gladly indeed. Everyone was delighted to see him. Diarmaid said to them, 'Why are you so glad to see me? I have only been gone three or four days at the most.'

Fionn looked at him and said, 'Diarmaid, you have been gone seven long years.'

From that time on Diarmaid never truly loved any other woman, but when a woman discovered the mark on his forehead she loved him. Diamaid became not only the most handsome, the bravest and the kindest of all the Fianna, but he also became the one most loved by women.

From this story in later years was developed one of the greatest stories of the knights of King Arthur. Diamaid became Sir Galahad in the story, the most gallant of knights. The cup of healing became the Holy Grail and the search for it involving the adventures was also incorporated into the Arthurian myth.

I was told this story originally by two old men in Ardnamurchan. They were two brothers who lived together and at the time of telling the story to me they were in their late 80s and I was about 12 years old.

The Sound of the Surge of the Sea – An Ataireachd Ard

HE WAS SEVEN YEARS of age and to him all the world was here in his sweet green glen in Lewis. Here he had everything he could ever want – his brother, his sisters, his playmates, his father and mother, the little house, the burn running down through the glen and the heather and the hills, where he can run and play with great delight. Above all came the sound of the surge of the sea.

He was only seven years of age. He did not understand when the bailiff came, and the soldiers, and told his mother and father they would have to leave by the big ship.

He was only seven years of age. He did not understand the great ship coming in from the bay and the small boats that came from it, and the people who were put into the small boats and taken out to the big ship. He thought this was some kind of treat for them and the ship would perhaps let them walk around on it; perhaps sail round the bay even.

He was only seven years of age. He did not understand. He could not realise why the older people around him were weeping and his father and mother too were greatly upset.

He was only seven years of age. He did not understand when they went on board the big ship and the big ship set sail. He thought they would sail out a bit, go round and come back to his dear sweet glen to hear again the sound of the surge of the sea.

He was only seven years of age. He did not understand when they were forced down below into the ship, into their accommodation which consisted of a bunk about six feet long and three feet wide for himself and his brother and his sisters and the same size for his mother and father.

He was only seven years of age. He could not understand. The ship sailed far out to sea and was tossed and wracked by wind and waves.

He was only seven years of age. He did not understand. He thought that somehow, sometime, the ship would turn around and sail back;

back to his sweet green glen in Lewis where he could listen to the sound of the surge of the sea.

Even when they reached the far land, the land of Newfoundland, where they were put ashore, he thought that somehow this was just a trip and that perhaps, once they were put ashore, they would go back onto the ship and sail back home.

He was only seven years of age. He did not understand when he and his brother, his two sisters, his mother and father trekked into the wilderness of Canada, trying to find a place for his father and mother to set up a small farm. He still did not understand.

As he grew up, they worked the land they had but it was not enough to keep them all and the day came when he had to move out; move away from the family home and find work elsewhere. Always the dream was in the back of his mind that someday, somehow he would return to his sweet green glen in Lewis and meet again there his companions, his friends of former years, and listen again to the sound of the surge of the sea.

He moved down into America and he worked in the great steel mills there, hard driven work. He lived as best he could, yet always in the back of his mind was the dream that someday, somehow he would return to his sweet green glen in Lewis.

Time passed as time does and it came to him one day that age was upon him and still he had not got back to his sweet green glen in Lewis. He gathered together what resources he had; he scraped together enough money for a passage back to Lewis. He sailed back and all the time in the back of his mind was this dream that had never left him of how he would be in his sweet green glen in Lewis and meet again with his companions to hear again the sound of the surge of the sea and happiness again would be theirs.

The ship reached Stornoway. He came off the ship and walked across Lewis to where his sweet green glen was but when he came to the glen realisation struck him, for there was no sound of children playing in the glen and the houses were mere ruins of walls. The only sound in the glen was the bleat of the sheep. But one thing remained, for over and above the bleating of the sheep he could hear the sound of the surge of the sea. He realised that for him there was nothing left, nothing at all here, none of his companions. All he could do was make certain that when he died his body would be buried in a knoll in his sweet green glen where he would be looking out over the sea and could hear forever the sound of the surge of the sea.

Many years later, one of the bards of Lewis heard this story, which was of one of his ancestors, and he put together the sound that it carried. The rhythm that the story carried he made into one of the great songs which are still sung.

the three feathers – *na tri h'itean*

HERE WAS A FARMER. He was a very good farmer, diligent with his crops and with his cattle, and he had good results from both. But he was a man who scoffed at the beliefs of that time. He would not leave out a little offering for the little people; he would not take part in the rituals and the ceremonies. The others warned him, 'You can't keep doing this. The little people will have their revenge upon you and you will be made to suffer.'

The farmer laughed at them and carried on as before. He gave no offering to the little people nor took part in the ceremonies. Everything seemed to go very well with him. His crops grew well, his cattle got good prices at the sales and everything was fine. So it went on for some years. The farmer and his wife and their son and daughter lived happily there and flourished, but still people said to him, 'Oh no, you may think the little people have forgotten about you or that they never existed, but the day will come when they will have their revenge upon you.'

The farmer would just laugh at the people telling him this. Of course he did not allow his son or his daughter or his wife take part in anything either.

Now one day, just about the time of *An Samhainn* – Halloween – the farmer, his wife and his two children were working down in the field when all of a sudden the *An Sluaghan*, the fairy host, came flying over the field. As it flew across they lifted the farmer's wife, son and daughter up into their midst and flew on with the farmer left behind, standing in his field. At first he thought it was some kind of trick that people had played upon him and his wife and children would come back, but the weeks went by and there was no sign of them. The month went by and there was no sign of them. The farmer was very distraught indeed for he dearly loved his wife and his children, so eventually he went to see the wise woman.

The wise woman said to him, 'The little people have taken their revenge by taking that which you loved most.'

The farmer said, 'But can I not get them back one way or another?'

'Yes, you can,' the wise woman said, 'but if you do it you will put yourself in great danger.'

The farmer said, 'I am not worried about the danger I put myself in. I'll do anything to get my wife and children back.'

'Then,' said the wise woman, 'This is what you must do. At *An Samhainn*, you must go to the top of the great cliff that towers above your farm. You must stand on the very edge of the cliff naked and facing to the West. Then you will see the fairy host rising as if from the bottom of the cliff and flying over your head, and in the midst of them will be your wife, son and your daughter. Your must take your dirk, which you will have with you, and swing it *deasil* (clockwise) three times around your head then hurl it into the midst of the fairy host, as close as you can to your wife and children.'

The farmer said, 'Is that what I must do?'

'That is it.' said the wise woman, 'That is what you must do.'

The farmer went back to his farm and he looked at the cliff. The cliff was very high and very steep and he knew that at the very top of it, the foothold was very precarious and he must stand at the very edge, looking down to where the sea crashed and roared on the rocks one thousand feet below. However, his love for his wife, son and daughter prevailed and at *An Samhainn* he went up the cliff and stood at the very edge, naked as nature had made him, and with him he took his dirk. After quite a time standing there he saw the fairy host rising from the base of the cliff and moving up. They flew over his head and in the midst of them he saw his wife, his son and his daughter. And as the wise woman had instructed him, he swung the dirk three times *deasil* around his head, although he wobbled a bit as he did it, and hurled it as close as he could to his wife, son and daughter.

There was a wild screeching and the fairy host disappeared. Down from the sky came drifting three feathers. The feathers landed beside him at the top of the cliff and as the feathers touched the ground they turned into his wife, his son and his daughter. They were all delighted to see each other again, to be back together. They went back down to the farmhouse and had a celebration to themselves there, but this time they did not forget to give something from the celebration to the little people. And from that time on the farmer and his wife and children never ever forgot to give something to the little people, and to join rituals and celebrations. And if the farmer was ever inclined to forget, all he had to do was to look at his wife, for across her cheek was a scar for the dirk had come so close to her.

I heard this story from old people in Ardnamurchan and also from old people in Mull and in Skye. None of them however wanted their names to be connected in any way with the story.

the last great clan battle

OW THE MACLEODS and the MacDonalds had been feuding for many, many years. The disputes flared up, died down and flared up again but at this time Ruaridh Mor MacLeod was trying to work out some kind of peace strategy, and as part of this he had contacted Dol Gorm of the MacDonalds. A contract was made that Dol Gorm should handfast with the sister of Ruaridh Mor. The handfasting was carried out, but Ruaridh Mor was horrified as by the end of the first year and a day his sister was sent back. She was tied backwards on a one eyed horse, led by a one eyed servant with a one eyed mongrel dog running behind it, and his sister was blind in one eye. Once Ruaridh Mor saw this, anger welled within him but he was a cunning strategist and he did not immediately charge into the MacDonald lands. He instead thought of ways to fight MacDonald and to get others to assist him in this.

Ruaridh Mor was away in Inverary talking

with the duke of Argyll, perhaps with the end of the two of them attacking the MacDonalds. Whilst he was away the MacDonalds sent a strong party into the MacLeod lands in Waternish and Dunvegan, lifted a large amount of cattle and went off with them. Ruaridh Mor's brother Alasdair immediately sent out the fiery cross, raising the clan of the MacLeods to chase after the MacDonalds. The MacDonalds, as was quite common, had taken the cattle to *Coire na Creiche* in the Cuillins. They took them there to divide them up between the ones who had taken part in the raid. Alasdair MacLeod decided to charge down upon them and wipe them out. But what Alasdair did not know that there was actually a larger party of the MacDonalds than he had thought, and more of the MacDonalds were hidden among the rocks and the heather in *Coire na Creiche*. When the MacLeods came charging down the coire, expecting to easily wipe out the MacDonalds, the hidden bowmen of the MacDonalds, who were famous for their bowman skills, rose from the heather and behind the rocks and launched a great shower of arrows into the bodies of the MacLeods.

The MacDonalds were great bowmen and

many of the MacLeods fell under that hail of arrows. The main battle began. Now the glen was no longer sounding to the lowing of the cattle. Instead there was a clash of steel on steel. All that could be heard in the glen was the clash and rasp of it and the dull sound of steel cutting through flesh and above all the clashing, the screams and the groans of the dying and wounded men carried through the glen. It was a terrible fight and blood flowed from both sides. Many men were killed from both sides. There was so much blood flowing that the small stream coming from the coire was called the Little Red Stream – *Allt Dearg Beag*. The big stream coming from the coire was called *Allt Dearg Mhor* – The Great Red Stream. Alasdair MacLeod and 30 of his men were taken prisoner by the MacDonalds. Some men could escape but there had been so much slaughter in this great fight that King James the VI decreed that there must be a peace made between the MacLeods and the MacDonalds. As part of this peace, Ruaridh Mor had to throw a great feast for the MacDonalds and the MacDonalds had to hand back to Ruaridh Mor his brother Alasdair MacLeod and the other prisoners. Ruaridh Mor was a sly man and he saw in this a way to eradicate the MacDonalds, because if he had them at the feast and sat one of the MacDonalds between two of his men at the feast, then at a given signal the MacDonalds could be killed.

The preparations for the great feast went ahead. Somehow the king heard of the plan and he sent word to Ruaridh Mor that if a single MacDonald died at the feast then Ruaridh Mor would be put to the horn, all his estates would be confiscated by the crown and he would never more be a chief in the Highlands. Under this threat Ruaridh Mor had to carry out the feast, perhaps through gritted teeth, perhaps not very happy. But the feast was carried out, the prisoners were exchanged and the two clans gave up their feud. The King also at this time made handfasting illegal throughout all Scotland, but although it was made illegal it still carried on to the middle of the 18th century.

This was the last clan battle because the things which the King had appointed were laid down not only upon the MacLeods and the MacDonalds but on every other clan in the whole of Scotland, and by this time the

King's might was so great that they knew he could take vengeance on them if they broke his laws, wherever they lived in Scotland.

Handfasting was a pre marriage co-habitation between a man and a woman for a year and a day. At the end of this time if there was no heir the man could return the woman to her family. If there was a heir then they must be married. In some cases the woman would not want to continue the union, but this was unusual. No stigma was attached to either party if the arrangement failed.

Brandon the Navigator

IN THE YEAR 500 AD or thereabouts, Brandon the Navigator had made all things ready in his boat built of leather stretched upon a frame built of timber to sail to the great land in the west, of which stories were told but which no man alive at that time had seen. Some before them had and had spoken of the beautiful land across the great ocean, a land that was young and hugely fertile. Although he had all the provisions he needed for the voyage, and the stores for repairs, he needed other men who were ready and experienced enough to encounter the stress of such a journey.

The men of Ireland were great enough sailors but they did not venture far from their own shores. This was his dilemma and he thought upon the ones most travelled by sea of all his compatriots. There were none who would have surpassed him in skills and experience. Then Brandon the Navigator thought of a man who had sailed all around to Ireland and to Scotland and around all the Isles of the Hebrides. He was now in Iona; Saint Columba himself, called Collum Cille.

Brandon, setting out in his boat came, after three days, to Iona and there on the shore to greet him was Collum Cille, standing on the beach below the abbey of Iona. The two men, each great in their own way, embraced and wished each other well.

'I have come', said Brandon, 'To ask that you, with your wisdom and knowledge of the sea and traversing of the sea, assist me in my voyage for which I have all I need except a crew.'

Saint Columba said he would think about the matter and pray for guidance, but in the meantime a meal was ready for all and after a night's sleep he would give an answer. When morning came Columba, true to his word, said to Brandon, 'I myself can't come with you on your voyage, although it would be a great pleasure for me, but I will give to you if you accept it three of those who will bring success in your venture, and with them my blessing.'

'More than that I could not wish.' said Brandon, and perhaps he was quite happy Columba could not go.

'This is what you must do,' said Columba.

'Sail from here, the isle of Iona, to Skye and from there to the small isle of *Flada Chuan*, where the fishermen go to wet the blue stone of the pagan sea-god.

'The third day you are there will come to the island a boat which will sail *deasil* (with the sun) three times around the island. The skipper of the boat will carry ashore water in a jug of brown earthenware which he will pour upon the stone. When he has done so say to him, 'Collum Cille says now is the voyage of your dreams. Come with me to my ship.' This man will be your helmsman for he is a man who can tell the way of a wave by a look, and how to ride it. He is a man fearless and at one with the sea, and already he has journeyed into the far north land which hurls out hot rocks, smoke and fire, but yet still he dreams of more.

'From that Island sail then to Tiree, *Eilean Eorna* (Isle of Barley). There upon the shore, beside the well, you will meet a tall man with eyes that blue they see through you. When you meet him, say to him 'The boat is ready and the helmsman on board but its master it lacks.' He will come with you and be your captain, for he is a man who can set the sails so that even the puffs of the wind from the wings of a dove will move the ship. He can tell by the touch of the wind and the smell of the sea the way to steer, and men will follow him even to the grave. When you sail from this Island you will take with you one of my monks; a man from Islay who can weave a song that man can row to and know no tiredness. The men will pull as he sings and he can charm any manner of men, whether his tongue is theirs or not. These are my gifts with my blessing for you.'

But Brandon said, 'Two of these men are worshippers of pagan gods. Can this be good on a ship which is of the one true god?'

'Is the ship good enough for the journey?' said Columba.

'She is indeed,' said Brandon.

'Then so are the men, for the same god made us all.'

So Brandon did as Columba said and of his voyage all men know.

Brandon was called the Navigator because he sailed round all the coast of Britain and

Ireland, yet always looked for more and greater lands across the sea and could navigate his way back to every place he visited.

He was later made into a Saint by the Roman Catholic church and named St Brendan.

The story of his journey to America and all his adventures are recorded in his journal of the voyage.

Hector the Fisherman – *Eachan an't Iasgair*

HECTOR AN'T IASGAIR was a fisherman. A fine figure of a man he was too, with his own boat, a head of black curly hair and a beard to match. He had a way with the girls that was a wonder to every other man in the glen and yet he was well liked by everyone for he had a pleasant easy way with everybody so that no one could fall out with him.

But in other ways he was a disaster. If Eachan planted potatoes, the blight would hit them, and if he cut hay, it would rain for a fortnight without stopping. And as a fisherman he was worse than all of Skye, so of course naturally he was the worst in the whole world. Eachan could go out the whole night fishing and come home with no fish, not even just one, when boats all around him would be pulling full nets. So of course he found it harder and harder to get a crew to get out with, for at that time the only pay would be what you caught, in an even division of the fish amongst the crew. One must admit it is a bit difficult to divide one fish between four, never mind none at all.

Eventually Eachan was left to go out on his own, but even then he caught more seaweed than fish. One night when Eachan was out alone on his boat he was a bit down, for though he appeared the same happy, easygoing young man, inside himself he was very depressed by his failures as a fisherman. All the other misfortunes that happened to him, like when he was milking, the cow kicked the stool from under him and made him spill the whole pail of milk; he could pass this off with a smile and a shrug. But his lack of ability as a fisherman really hurt, for it was the one thing that he wanted to be best at.

Full of his own thoughts, he left the other boats and headed for an area of the sea that was never fished by them for they said there were no fish there. But Eachan thought to himself, 'Well I can't catch fish where they are, so I might as well try were they aren't.'

Now he hadn't been fishing ten minutes when he felt a heavy pull in the net and started to haul it aboard. When the net was near the surface he saw that there was just one fish, but it was a giant. Full of hope and excitement he hauled it up and on to the deck of his boat but when he looked again, the fish was no longer there but instead a most beautiful girl tangled in his net. He hurried to get the net off her and when she was free of it she sat up right on the deck. Naked she was, with long hair the colour of golden seaweed flowing down her back and a slim lithe body with small firm breasts and long straight legs. Eachan fell in love on the spot for about the hundredth time. 'Well well,' says he, 'Were you out for a swim? You must have swam a long way.'

The girl just looked at him with her soft brown eyes and said nothing.

'I hope I didn't hurt you by pulling you up in my net.' said Eachan. 'But indeed I thought you were a big fish I caught.'

'I am no fish.' said the girl. 'Please put me back into the water.'

'Ah', said Eachan, 'I know the difference between a fish and a girl, but I won't be putting you back in, you are too far out. You could drown before you get back to the shore.'

'Please put me back!' she pleaded, 'I am getting dry, then I will catch a cold and get ill.'

Well, Eachan was not a man to see a girl shivering and himself with a jacket on. He had the jacket off in a flash and put it around her shoulders. To his surprise she tried to pull it off saying, 'Don't do that. I can't be dry and warm. Please, put me back or at least throw some water over me.'

Well now this made Eachan think of the stories he heard from the old folk in the glen and looking well again at the girl he said. 'No ordinary girl would ask for such a thing or swim so far. Tell me who you are and what you are.'

'I am called different names.' she said. 'Some call me *Nighean Mara* (Seamaid) or *Bidse Mara* (Whore of the Sea); some *Earasaighe* (Sea bitch) and some much worse.'

'I have heard of you right enough.' said Eachan. 'I also know that you are cursed and called the murderess of sailors and fishermen such as myself, but I cannot believe that anyone so beautiful can kill anyone.'

'That is true.' said she. 'So put me back into the sea and no harm will come to you.'

'I have also heard you can make a man the greatest fisherman in all the world.' said Eachan. 'I wish this from you or I will not put you back.'

'That gift you can have, but from this day on you must be true to me only and forsake all your women of the land.' said she.

'Gladly will I do that.' said Eachan, 'For being the best fisherman is my only dream.' With those words he lifted her to put her back into the water. As he did so she gave him a salt tasting kiss and slid into the water. Looking back she cried to him, 'Cast your net now and you and I will meet again, but you must fish alone.'

Eachan cast his net and in a moment it was so full that he could hardly haul it aboard. It was the biggest catch he had ever seen. When he reached the land with his boat nearly sinking with the weight of fish aboard, the people were astounded that Eachan, Hector the Fishless as he was called, Eachan *An't Iasgair*, had made such a catch. However, they said and thought that this was just one lucky catch for him and he would soon be back to his old ways. Eachan kept fishing by himself and all that season he had the best catches anyone could remember. Many now wanted to fish with him, but he would allow no one. The girls who had flocked about him also found him changed, for he who had loved them all now met with none. Some even said he was so much in love with the fishing he had turned into a cold fish himself, with no human feelings.

Eachan himself was happy. He was now hailed as the best fisherman in Skye, so of course also the best in the world, and unknown to the ones ashore, the *Bidse Mara* met him out at sea and came aboard his boat, sating his flames of passion. Yet things change, and as it came to the end of the season Eachan found himself falling out of love with his lady of the sea. He was always wet and cold when they made love, and although her passion was as great as his, sometimes he found himself comparing her unfavourably with some he had known ashore.

On the last fishing trip of the year Eachan felt safe enough in his new position as top fisherman that he decided he could do without the sea nymph. Besides that he had fallen head over heels for a red haired temptress and had promised to marry her. He sailed out and cast his net as usual and as he did so his sea nymph appeared beside the boat. Eachan leaned over the side as usual to lift her aboard but she linked an arm around his neck and pulled him into the water. Later that day, other fishing boats saw his boat lying rocking in the waves and when they went aboard there was no sign of Eachan. They pulled the nets which were still set and in the nets they found the body of Eachan with his arms wrapped around the biggest and strangest fish they had ever seen.

amadan domhnallach – macdonald's fool

N THE CASTLE of Camus stood MacDonald of Sleat and in his mind were dark and gloomy thoughts of defeat and flight from his beloved Skye. This very day a messenger had come to him from his guardians of the shores, the MacAskills, and black indeed was their news. Down upon them from the sea at Camus Ban had come the *Lochlannaich*. As they leapt ashore from their wooden horses the mighty fighting men of the MacAskills, the second best bodyguards in all of Skye had met them with sword and shield, spear and arrow, and had held them and started to drive them back to their boats. But when the battle was at its height and started to go the way of the MacAskills, Callain, chief of *Lochlannaich*, released upon them his personal bodyguard of berserkers with their great two edged war axes, and brave and good as were the MacAskills, the slaughter amongst them was so great that even they had broken and fled. Especially so as, the messenger said, the berserkers could not be killed, although many of them were sorely wounded; so much that blood splashed from every pore, yet they continued fighting and slaying. MacDonald called all his advisers to him for he knew that on the morrow he would need to lead his army and the remnants of the MacAskills against the *Lochlannaich* and those fearsome, unkillable berserkers. Many strategies were discussed to find a way to overcome them but not one of his captains could come up with a plan that showed any sign of success. The final plan was no plan at all but to get ready to fight and die as men should.

Now in the house of MacDonald lived an *Amadan* – a fool. He came forward and proposed to MacDonald the plan of a fool. He said that he had talked well with the messenger and only one berserker had been killed, and him by accident. In charging forward the berserker had fallen over the body of a clansman and while he was down another clansman cut off his head with a single blow of the two-handed claymore. Other berserkers had been stabbed with spears and swords, and had their limbs and chests laid open by axe and sword slashes, but none of them had died. It was evident that the only way to kill them was to cut off their heads but that was much easier to say than to do.

Yet the Amadan believed that he had the answer in his plan. The plan was simple. When the MacDonalds marched on to Camus Ban next day the front line would form a screen and behind them several men with ropes would lie on the ground as if dead, with the ropes running between them under the grass or sand. When the berserkers charged upon the front line, the MacDonalds would fight briefly but then turn and run. The berserkers in their fighting fury would charge after them and then the dead bodies would pull the ropes taut, tripping the berserkers up. At the same time other seemingly dead men would rise up with their two-handed claymores and behead the berserkers. The captains were not much impressed with what they considered was the plan only a fool would form, but MacDonald said it was better than any put forward by them and they would act upon it.

The next day MacDonald, at the head of his men, marched on to Camus Ban and they were attacked by the *Lochlannaich* but took

the initial thrust of the invaders without giving ground. Then the berserkers charged. And as the Amadan had planned, after a brief but bloody resistance the front-line broke and fled. Howling their bloodlust the berserkers charged on, only to fall over the ropes pulled taut among their legs, and every one of them was beheaded before they could rise. Now the army of MacDonald charged upon the remains of the Lochlannaich and those few who reached the ships sailed away to lick their wounds.
The bodies of the berserkers were gathered together and buried at the top of the bay and the heads were buried elsewhere.

It is a wise man who knows when to listen to a fool.

the Boat – am Bata

MY GRANDUNCLE John was a man who was held in awe by a lot of the people in the village. It was claimed of him that he was fey, that he had correspondence with the little people, had strange powers, but my grandaunt used to say of him that he was just a clown who couldn't keep his hands in his pocket, as they say. Now on this occasion he had gone to a sale in Fort William. He had taken two cattle beasts with him to be sold and my aunt had warned him well that he was to come back from the sale with nothing except the money for the beasts.

John went to the sale and at the sale the beasts were sold. He got a good price for them and was quite happy. He remembered what his wife had told him and kept the money in his pocket, but as he was walking back down to the shore in Fort William he saw an old man sitting in a boat. It was a good boat and as John walked down the old man said to him, 'I am selling this boat. Would you like to buy it?'

John looked at the boat and said, 'Well, perhaps I would.' For suddenly, as he looked at the boat, he saw a blue light at the top of the mast and as he watched the blue light ran down, down to the bow sprit.

John said to the old man, 'How much do you want for the boat?'

The old man said to him, 'What have you got in your pockets from the sales?'

John took out of his pocket what he had got for the cattle at the sales and said, 'Yes, I will give you all of it for this boat, for I know this boat has a task to perform.'

The old man took the money and handed half of the money back to John as a luckspenny. John took the money and the boat and he got a friend to help him. Together they sailed the boat right down to past the point of Ardnamurchan to below the waterfall at Lochshiel, where they took it on to the beach. When John went up home to his house in Shielfoot his wife told him off thoroughly for buying a boat he didn't really need, and also for having only half of the money from the sale. But John said, 'That boat, it has something to do; something that concerns myself.'

And from that time on, he would watch the boat. Sometimes he would go out on it.

It needed four men to row it but it had mast and sail as well. They would go out in it, fish from it and catch fish. John would look at the boat and he would see the blue light at the top of the mast. Although his wife would hardly admit it, sometimes she too saw the blue light at the top of the mast.

Time moved on and the war started. John one day in the evening was looking down at the boat and saw the blue light on the mast and, as he watched, it rolled down the mast, right down to the very tip of the bow sprit. John then knew the time had come for the boat's task. He called on four friends of his and they went down to the boat, got it into the sea and sailed out. As they sailed, John could see the blue light no longer in the bow sprit but dancing ahead of the boat. They followed the light and they sailed out and out to where the sea was very rough, and after some time the men started to say that they should turn back but John said, 'No, we must continue. We must keep on and the light will lead us.'

They came to a spot in the sea when the light suddenly came back towards the boat, and as it did so they caught sight of someone floating in the sea, holding on to a large junk of timber. They got across to the person with difficulty and managed to pull the person into the boat, then they headed back to the shore. The sea was very rough now, very rough indeed, but they carried on their way and fought against wind and wave until they reached the beach below the waterfall of the river Shiel. When they reached the beach they looked at the man and the man was a cousin of John. He was able to tell them that his ship had been blown up out past Ardnamurchan Point and he was the only one it seems who had managed to get to safety. John after that kept the boat on the beach but there were no longer strong men left in the village to row it out to sea, and the blue light had disappeared from the top of the mast. John knew that the task of the boat had been fulfilled and he was happy that he had bought the boat.

The Minister and the Evils of Drink

THERE WAS A MINISTER and he was a very good minister. He attended to his congregation, he preached well on the Sabbath and everyone agreed that he was indeed a very good minister.

He visited the sick and he did everything a good minister should do but he had a fly in the ointment. Old Sandy was a man that the minister knew liked to go on a ceilidh on a Saturday night, drink very well indeed and then on a Sunday, there he would be, in the church sitting in the pew. The minister's problem was that as soon as he started his sermon Sandy's head would go down, his eyes would close and they would not open again until the end of the sermon.

The minister could not work out whether this was Sandy sleeping off the excesses of the night before or closing his eyes and putting his head down to concentrate more thoroughly on the sermon. The minister decided he would need to do something about it. So the following

Sabbath he had a great sermon. Oh, a very good sermon indeed. It was all about the evils of drink and how you should avoid them and at the very peak of his sermon he reached under the pulpit and brought out two jars. The minister held the jars up and said, 'Now my beloved brethren, you will have noticed that in my right hand there is a jar filled with water with a worm in it and in my left hand there is a jar with whisky and a worm in it. You will have noticed, my beloved brethren, that the worm in the jar of water is quite happily swimming about but the worm in the jar of whisky is dead. Now, beloved brethren, what does this prove?'

At that point old Sandy's head came up, his eyes shot open and his voice boomed out over the church, 'Minister, it proves if you drink whisky you won't have worms!'

The People from Under the Sea – *An Lochlannaich*

DEEP, DEEP DOWN in the depths of the great sea, where peace dwelled and the dark green gloom was pierced by no shaft of light from the world above, lived a race of people who had their own world and culture and way of life, which paralleled that of the land yet was not of it.

They were the people from beneath the sea, the *Lochlannaich*, and they had been a great and strong people. The evidence of their great skills and high cultural achievements was all around them in the great marble palaces in which they lived; the magnificent arches and towering columns carved in intricate designs. Yet when Lachlan, the great king of the Lochlannaich, looked around he realised that the powers of the people from under the sea were fading, as powers do. The powers were fading especially quickly since they had invaded the lands of the sons of Morna. Fionn had come across to defend the sons of Morna and had inflicted a very heavy defeat upon the *Lochlannaich*. Now as Lachlan looked around he saw that their powers to hold back the water were fading fast. His great cities below the sea might soon be engulfed and washed away. His people too were growing less in number.

Lachlan called his people together and he said to them that they had tried time and again to establish a place above the sea, a place on the land where they could settle and live, but they had not succeeded in this at all. He told them now was the time to use a different way of establishing themselves and he said to them, 'You who are young and fit amongst us must go and merge into the people of the land. You must adopt their ways and live with them as if you were of them, but there will always remain with you a part of your own life under the sea.'

The people listened to Lachlan and they went away. Some of them went up unto the land, young and fit women and men. The women were very easily accepted amongst the people of the land because they were tall, slim girls with full breasts and narrow waists, wide childbearing hips and long elegant legs. The men of the land were more than willing to accept them. But the men of the *Lochlannaich* were not so easily accepted. They were short, rather squat built, dark haired and not of prepossessing features. One or two managed to salvage themselves but the rest were flung out and rejected, and had to return in despair to the land under the sea. One or two of the girls found that they did not like life on the land and they too returned to the land of the *Lochlannaich*. When they returned Lachlan said to them, 'You have failed, but rather than have you go with the rest of us here I will make you into creatures of both sea and land.'

Lachlan turned the men and women into seals, and as seals the people from under the sea swam back to the shore, but to some of them he gave the power to change back to women or men and also the power to move on land, as to mix still with the men and women of the land. Some of these *Lochlannaich* people would come to land to live permanently, to merge with the men and woman of the land and to carry offspring. This offspring would later become known by the people as fearless sailors and great swimmers. They were accepted by the people of the land as that.

The ones of the people from under the sea who could only come to the land for a short time also had offspring; some by the people of the land, and from them there came a race who were known as not only great swimmers, great navigators and great seamen, but also people who were great masons and sculptors and very, very fond indeed of the land. They too split into different races eventually, and from them were descended the MacPhees of Colonsay, the MacCodrums of Uist and the MacKinnons of Skye. To this very day, if you look amongst these races you will find that many of them are exceptionally good swimmers or seamen, and all have a very great love for the land.

But down in the great marble halls of the *Lochlannaich* time had moved on. The waters came in and washed over the great marble palaces and the Lochlannaich and their palaces were washed away. Still, the palaces remained as ruins under the sea for people from the land to find and wonder about, because no one really knows where the people of the sea went to.

There are many stories in the Scottish and the Gaelic culture of people from below the sea and some of these stories speak also of the beautiful marble cities. It is also noted that stories of mermaids and seals also carry in them the joining and the merging between the people of the land and the sea, and the progeny from all these meetings being noted for their prowess at sea.

lochlannaich – the people from below the sea

This is a slightly different version of that story as told before. I am never sure of which one is the best.

OW THE LOCHLANNAICH had tried many, many times to establish for their race a place on land where they could live. They had attacked the people of the land on many occasions but they had not been successful and on their very last expedition, against the sons of Morna, they had been defeated very badly, for the sons of Morna called upon Fionn to come and help them. Fionn had come and destroyed the *Lochlannaich* and now they had retreated in great disorder to their marble cities below the sea.

Lachlan, the king of the *Lochlannaich*, looked about and consulted his elders for he could see the powers of the *Lochlannaich* were waning and their numbers too were decreasing all the time. Lachlan called the council of the elders to see if they could find a solution to this decreasing of numbers and the loss of their powers. Lachlan knew that eventually they would reach a time when their powers would be so worn away that the sea would take over and come crashing in upon the palaces and houses in there. All that would be left would be devastation, wailing and weeping, but there would be no answer for their destiny.

Lachlan and his elders decided that the only solution was to merge quietly with the people of the earth, of the land. It would have to be done very secretly, without any fighting, and to this end Lachlan called together all the young men and women of the *Lochlannaich*. He said to them, 'You, to save our race, must go and meet with the people of the land and be as they are and live with them and carry their children.'

The young people of the Lochlannaich swam ashore and merged with the people of the earth. Now this was not a hard job for the young women of the Lochlannaich for they were tall, slim, full breasted and slim-waisted with wide childbearing hips and long beautiful legs and faces of beautiful complexion. It was no problem for them to meet up with the men of the land and be with them and have children by them. But the men of the *Lochlannaich* found it much more difficult for they were rather short, squat built with rather ugly features and black hair. Nonetheless some of them managed to live with the women of the land. Those men that could not merge with the women on the land, and several of the women of the *Lochlannaich* who could not bear to stay on the land, returned to the sea, to the great white city. There Lachlan told them that they had failed; failed in their duty to save the race of the *Lochlannaich*. But because they had tried, he would grant them something of their mortality and he turned them there and then into seals. To some of the seals he gave the power that they were able to return to the land and walk on the land, to merge with the people of the land, but they must always return to the sea in due course.

Some of the woman he turned into mermaids and they too could walk and merge with the people of the land, but they too had to return to the sea in due course. They could not stay away from it for any long length of time. Now the people of the *Lochlannaich* did merge with the people of the land and they had many children, both male and female. From these children came tribes of the land who were noted for their great prowess on sea. They were great swimmers, great boatmen and great navigators and people looked up to them. Sometimes the people of the land gave a hint that they knew that these people had come from the sea. For the different tribes were marked as different persons from the sea. They were called the sons of the *Lochlannaich* and they were noted for their prowess in all the things involving the sea. Eventually they split into clans and were named. One of them were the MacPhees of Colonsay, another were the MacCodrums of Uist and another the MacKinnons of Skye. They were never highly numerous but they were there.

These clans were famed and accepted for their knowledge of the sea, but their relations, the old people, who had been left in the cities below the sea, knew only death and destruction, for the powers of the people from below the sea ebbed away until the sea took over. As Lachlan the king had said, the waters crashed in upon the white cities, bringing with them destruction and death to the people from under the sea and their beautiful marble palaces. The cities are still there below the sea and people from time to time find those cities and wonder about the great beauty and the power of the builders of them, but they know not who the builders were.

Of those clans, the MacPhees, the MacKinnons and MacCodrums, there are still some today who are noted for their great prowess at swimming and all the things with the sea. One of the descendants of the MacPhees of Colonsay was Collum Cille himself, St Columba. He was proud to boast that he was of the people from below the sea for his grandmother was a MacPhee of Colonsay.

The first version of this story is of Skye and Uist. The second version is from Argyllshire and it would appear to be a slightly later version than the first.

The Flying Barrel

MY GRANDUNCLE John was a cooper in the gun powder factory in Kames in Argyll. He worked there for a long number of years. In one of his accounts of the most interesting days in the Cooperage, the Copperage reinstated gun powder barrels brought back by the forces.

On this occasion barrels had been brought back and the standard procedure was to take the bung out of the head of the barrel, pour water into the barrel and wash the inside of it well, so that any residue of the gun powder would be washed out or made inert. To take out the bung they would use a copper chisel type and a copper headed hammer so no sparks would be occasioned. This time it was one of the smaller barrels; a firking it was called. It had been brought back and it had to be checked as usual to decide whether it was fit for usage or needed repairs.

There was a young apprentice in the Cooperage at this time who decided he could not wait for somebody else to open the barrel and he would take the bung out by himself.

But unfortunately instead of using the copper spike and the copper hammer, he picked up an iron spike and hammer and started to batter the spike into the bung. He succeeded in starting to open the bung, but as he did so sparks from the hammer and spike ignited the powder inside the barrel. The barrel sailed off the barrel bench with a great roar, like a rocket as my granduncle put it. The barrel was roaring down through the factory, swerving upwards, out through the roof, landing on the beach and shattered into a thousand fragments.

The only one hurt by this incident was the young apprentice himself. He was not badly hurt, only slightly burnt, but he never ever finished his apprenticeship.

mermaids – *maighdean mhara*

WHEN THE MERMAIDS first came from under the sea they were just like any people in the land. They could walk about on the land the same as anybody else and they were very beautiful girls; tall, full breasted and slim waisted, with wide childbearing hips and long slim elegant legs. They were so beautiful that they could have any of the men of the land they wished to. But the women of the land were very annoyed by this because these mermaids would approach their sons or their husbands, whatever the mermaids fancied. They had no objections whatsoever to whether the person they went to bed with was married or a young lad.

The women of the land decided to appeal to the god of the sea and ask him to do something on their behalf. The god of the sea heard what they had to say and he called the mermaids in front of him and reprimanded them. He told them they would have to stop doing this, as this was wrong, and the mermaids promised they would mend their ways. Unfortunately however, the mermaids did not last long in this and soon were back to their old ways of enticing the men from the land, regardless of who they were.

Once again the women of the land appealed to the god of the sea, and the god of the sea again called the mermaids in front of him. He told them that they had not kept their promises and because of this he was going to make it that they could not be on the land as in the sea. There and then he gave each of the mermaids in place of their legs a large, scaly tail. When the mermaid realised they could not go on the land they were very annoyed by this, but they swam out to Ardnamurchan Point and they sat.

When they saw a ship nearing they would show themselves to the men on the ship and shout to them and sing to them. The men on the ship would come in closer to have a better look and very often the ship would be wrecked. The mermaids would pick from the swimming men the ones they fancied and they would have their time with them and then throw them back to the water again. They did not go on the land, so the sea god could do nothing about it, and the mermaids are there on Ardnamurchan Point, and several other points around the coast of Scotland now, and people have heard of them for many years and the sailors still dread the thought of meeting up with the mermaids, for they know it brings only death.

Seamus and the Monster

SEAMUS WAS AN OLD retired sailor who lived in Millhouse in Argyll. He was a man full of stories of the sea, especially about the times when he worked on the whaling ships – some of which were regarded with suspicion. One of his favourites was a story about a great sea monster. He would always start off with 'Well you know, boys, I was never a man to believe in all those stories about sea monsters but I had to change my tack after this happened to me.

'We were off the coast of South Africa after the sperm whales and as you know it was the sailing boats in those days and when the lookout in the crows nest would cry out, we would get into the whaling boats, eight of us into one boat – six to row, a harpooner in the bows and a helmsman at the stern. We would row in the direction of the blowing. The man in the crows nest would point directions to us and when we got to the side of the whales, we would get as close as we could and the harpooner would choose the moment to put the harpoon in the whale. Those harpooners seldom missed. The rope from the harpoon would go roaring out as the whale sounded. Sometimes it would go out so fast we had to throw water over it to stop it burning the hawse-hole. Then when the whale came to it and up towards the boat again the harpooner would shoot another harpoon into it and we would ram spears into its sides if we were close enough. It was a bloody business and the sea around the boat would be red with blood.

'Now this time, as we were rowing across towards the whale the harpooner was just getting ready to fire the harpoon when all of a sudden, out of nowhere a great arm came across the stern of the boat and knocked the helmsman clean into the water. Then other arms came round the stern and the boat was starting to sink, and at the same time out of the sea came the great monster. Right in the centre of the body of the monster we could see a huge beak like a parrot's beak, but 50 times bigger on the monster and it was drawing us towards it. It was the harpooner that saved us, who picked up the sharp axe that was kept in the boat in case you had to cut the rope, and he hacked off the first arm and bits of the others. The monster retreated from the stern and the sea turned black as the monster dived down into it.

'We rowed back to the ship, as did the other boats. We never found the helmsman but when we got to the ship they had seen too what just happened and took us aboard and gave each of us a good dram of rum. The skipper entered the incident into the log but as soon as we downed our drams he sent us back to catch the whales. At the end of the voyage, I signed off and came back home here. I have never been on the sea since. We had measured the arm of the sea monster we hacked off back at the ship and it was over 14 feet long, but I do not know what happened to it then, nor do I want to know.'

the ship that died for love

SOME YEARS AGO a young man who had been blacklisted by the shipping companies because he refused to take part in the eviction of crofters decided to start a ferry service between Lewis, the Outer Isles in general and Skye.

He got a ship and started his service. It was mainly cattle he ferried and sheep, but he was doing very well at it. Eventually he was across at Stornaway and he met a very beautiful girl. They fell in love and were to be married.

The skipper sailed his ship and on one trip he left Skye, went across from Lewis to Stornaway, and the girl this time asked him to take her with him, to take her back to Skye with him. He said no because he believed that they should not be together in a permanent way until they were married. He believed in the chastity of marriage. The girl pleaded with him but he would not consent. He sailed back to Skye without the girl but with a load of sheep and cattle.

After he got back to Skye, the ship was unloaded and then reloaded with stuff to go to Lewis like wool and other things. Off he went on his ship and when his ship arrived in Stornaway he was met by the dreadful news that the girl who was to be married to him had died of a fever which had been brought into Stornaway by a foreign ship. The skipper of the ship was mad with grief when he heard this about his beloved. He blamed himself because he had not given in to her and taken her back to Skye with him. But once again the ship was loaded and he sailed back to Skye.

When they came back to Skye, the ship came into Dunvegan Pier and the cattle were unloaded. The skipper then sailed the ship out towards where his moorings usually were. He sailed the ship out himself and the crew accepted this because it had been done before; the skipper and sometimes one of the crew would sail the ship the short distance to its mooring. On this occasion however the skipper sailed out, there was a strong snoring breeze, and as the crew watched him sailing out they realised he was not going to the mooring. He sailed further out, brought the ship round and headed straight for the shore. With the big wind that was blowing the ship gained great speed. It hurtled in towards the shore and the skipper stood there steering it. The ship reached the shore at the little bay before Claigan (The Place of the Skull) and so great was his speed at the moment of impact that the ship drove right upon the shore, almost out of the water. The mast crashed over and killed the skipper and the boat was stranded there at the shore of Claigan.

Up to a few years ago you could go down to Claigan and you could see the remains of the rotten hull of the ship stranded up on the shore. Not one of the local people took so much as a piece of timber from the ship, although it could have helped them in many ways. In more recent years people – walkers, hikers, etc. – have been down through Claigan and have lit fires near the ship and used the ships timbers for their fires. Now all that is left of the ship that died for love is the keel, part metal, part wood, buried just above the high water mark.

The Loch of the Grey Wolf – *Loch Madadh Glaseachd*

IN ARDNAMURCHAN THERE is a Loch called *Loch Madadh Glaseachd*, the Loch of the Grey Wolf. The reason it was called this was that, at that time, beside the loch there lived a great grey wolf. And this grey wolf was a very savage animal. It roamed around the loch; it took lambs, it took young calves and the thing that was the tastiest of all to it was young children. Hunters came and tried to kill the wolf but the wolf always managed to evade them, to escape, and they could not kill it or catch it. Eventually it was decided the best thing to do was to leave the area of the loch bare and allow the wolf to roam there.

Not far from the loch there dwelled an old lady. She had a small cottage on a little piece of ground. She had very little but one day her daughter asked the old lady if she would look after her two children as she had to go away for a while. The old lady of course said yes, she would look after the children. She took the children in but the problem was feeding them, for the old lady had very little. It was the time of year however when the blaeberries grew thickly in the hillsides and the old lady and the children gathered the blaeberries. The old lady made them into pies, oatmeal crumbles; she made and prepared the blaeberries in many different ways to serve them up to the children so they ate quite well. But before very long the blaeberries round about her house and the adjoining countryside had been used up by the old lady and her grandchildren. The old lady reached a stage where she was left with nothing for the children to eat and she wondered what on earth she would do. She knew that near the Loch of the Grey Wolf there grew blaeberries in profusion, and she decided that what she would have to do was to go with the children and gather the blaeberries there, near the loch.

They set off with baskets, reached the loch and started to gather the blaeberries. They gathered the blaeberries and there was no sign of the grey wolf. The old lady was beginning to think that, 'Well, we are going to have the baskets full, we will get them back to the house and the grey wolf won't have been near us at all.'

Just as she was thinking this, from nowhere appeared the great grey wolf. He hurtled down the hillside straight towards the children and they could see his great jaws open wide, the fierce fangs within the jaws and the saliva dribbling from them. But as he came charging for the children, the old lady jumped between the children and the wolf. As she jumped between them, she took off her apron and wrapped it around her hand and arm, then she thrust the apron and her arm straight down the wolf's mouth, down into his throat as far as she could, and held it there. The wolf thrashed about; threw her from side to side trying to get rid of this old woman and her choking arm, but the old lady, in spite of the her arm being torn and lacerated below his teeth, kept the arm and the apron down the wolf's throat and eventually the wolf weakened and died. When the old lady was sure the wolf was dead, only then she took from his throat her arm and her apron. And that was how the last wolf of Ardnamurchan was killed by an old lady and her apron.

the factor of kilchoan

AT KILCHOAN IN ARDNAMURCHAN the factor was a very cruel young man. He was not seen to have any mercy in him. He was cold and ruthless and he wanted to get rid of all the crofters so that his master, the laird, could rent the land around Kilchoan for sheep farming.

Now the big ship came into the bay of Kilchoan and the soldiers and the bailiffs and the factor came into Kilchoan and started to evict the crofters. They evicted all the crofters and as they did so they burned the thatch above their heads so that they could not come back to the cottage they had stayed in for generations, even if they wanted to. There was one cottage however, and in it there lived a very old lady, and when the soldiers and the bailiffs came into the house and saw the state she was in; how old, weak and frail she was, not even they would take her out to take her down to the boats. The soldiers refused to take her out and the officer in charge refused to order his men to do it. But when the factor came along he said even if they would not do it, he would do it

himself. He went into the cottage, picked the old lady up in his arms and carried her down to the boat, threw her down into the stern sheet of the boat and she was rowed out to the big ship. But as she was thrown into the stern sheets of the boat she looked at the factor and put a curse upon him. She told the factor that old as she was and weak as she was, and young and strong as he was, he would die before her. And when he died and was buried he, his soul, would go straight to hell and the sign of this would be that on his grave would grow nothing but nettles and bindweed for ever more.
The factor laughed at her and carried on.

Strange as it may seem, the old lady survived the journey across to Novascotia and lived for some time there, but the factor, just a few weeks after the ship sailed, died very suddenly with no obvious cause for his death. His body was buried in Kilchoan cemetery and when the earth and the turf had settled down again and started to grow, there grew on his grave nothing but bindweed and nettle. And if you go to Kilchoan cemetery this very day, you will see in the cemetery a grave which is fenced around with wrought iron and inside the wrought iron nothing grows but bindweed and nettles. The relations of the factor tried on several occasions to remove the bindweed and nettles, to replace them with other plants. They even scooped the surface of the earth out of the grave and the turf, to replace it with other turf and other earth, but no matter what they did, as soon as the grave settled, back again came the bindweed and the nettles. And as I said, they are still there to this very day.

Some other books published by **LUATH** PRESS

Luath Storyteller: Highland Myths and Legends

George W Macpherson
ISBN 1 84282 064 8 PBK £5.99

The mythical, the legendary, the true – this is the stuff of stories and story-tellers, the preserve of Scotland's ancient oral tradition.

Celtic heroes, fairies, Druids, selkies, sea horses, magicians, giants and Viking invaders – these tales have been told round campfires for centuries and are now told here today. Some of George Macpherson's stories are over 2,500 years old. Strands of these timeless tales cross over and interweave to create a delicate tapestry of Highland Scotland as depicted by its myths and legends.

Luath Storyteller: Tales of Loch Ness

Stuart McHardy
ISBN 1 906307 59 8 PBK £5.99

We all know the Loch Ness Monster. Not personally, but we've definitely heard of it. Stuart McHardy knows a lot more stories about Loch Ness monsters, fairies and heroes than most folk, and he has more than a nodding acquaintance with Nessie, too.

From the lassie whose forgetful-ness created the loch to St Columba's encounter with a rather familiar sea-monster nearly 1,500 years ago, from saints to hags to the terrible *each-uisge*, the waterhorse that carries unwitting riders away to drown and be eaten beneath the waters of the loch, these tales are by turns funny, enchanting, gruesome and cautionary. Derived from both history and legends, passed by word of mouth for untold generations, they give a glimpse of the romance and glamour, the danger and the magic of the history of Scotland's Great Glen.

Story provided the people of the ancient tribes with their education, their self-awareness and their understanding of the world they inhabited.

STUART MCHARDY

Luath Storyteller: Tales of the Picts

Stuart McHardy
ISBN 1 84282 097 4 PBK £5.99

For many centuries the people of Scotland have told stories of their ancestors, a mysterious tribe called the Picts. This ancient Celtic-speaking people, who fought off the might of the Roman Empire, are perhaps best known for their Symbol Stones – images carved into standing stones left scattered across Scotland, many of which have their own stories. Here for the first time these tales are gathered together with folk memories of bloody battles, chronicles of warriors and priestesses, saints and supernatural beings. From Shetland to the Border with England, these ancient memories of Scotland's original inhabitants have flourished since the nation's earliest days and now are told afresh, shedding new light on our ancient past.

Luath Storyteller: Tales of Edinburgh Castle

Stuart McHardy
ISBN 1 905222 95 5 PBK £5.99

Who was the new-born baby found buried inside the castle walls?

Who sat down to the fateful Black Dinner?

Who was the last prisoner to be held in the dungeons of Edinburgh Castle, and what was his crime?

Towering above Edinburgh, on the core of an extinct volcano, sits a grand and forbidding fortress.

Edinburgh Castle is one of Scotland's most awe-inspiring and iconic landmarks. A site of human habitation since the Bronze Age, the ever-evolving structure has a rich and varied history and has been of crucial significance, militarily and strategically, for many hundreds of years.

Tales of Edinburgh Castle is a salute to the ancient tradition of storytelling and paints a vivid picture of the castle in bygone times, the rich and varied characters to whom it owes its notoriety, and its central role in Scotland's history and identity.

The Supernatural Highlands

Francis Thompson

ISBN 0 946487 31 6 PBK £8.99

An authoritative exploration of the otherworld of the Highlander, happenings and beings hitherto thought to be outwith the ordinary forces of nature. A simple introduction to the way of life of rural Highland and Island communities, this new edition weaves a path through second sight, the evil eye, witchcraft, ghosts, fairies and other supernatural beings, offering new sightlines on areas of belief once dismissed as folklore and superstition.

Excellent guidebook to the Gaelic-speaking underworld.
THE HERALD

Tall Tales from an Island

[Mull]

Peter Macnab

ISBN 0 946487 07 3 PBK £8.99

Peter Macnab was reared on Mull, as was his father, and his grandfather before him, He heard many of these tales as a lad, and others he has listened to in later years. Although collected on Mull, these tales could have come from any one of the Hebridean islands. They are timeless and universal, and they are the tales still told round the fireside when the visitors have all gone home.

There are humorous tales, grim tales, witty tales, tales of witchcraft, tales of love, tales of heroism, tales of treachery, historical tales and tales of yester-year. There are unforgettable characters like Do'l Gorm, and philosophical roadman, and Calum nan Croig, the Gaelic storyteller whose highly developed art of convincing exaggeration mesmer-ised his listeners. There is a headless horseman, and a whole coven of witches. Heroes, fools, lairds, herdsmen, lovers and liars, dead men and live cats all have a place in this entrancing collection.

Tales of the North Coast

Alan Temperley

ISBN 0 946487 18 9 PBK £8.99

Seals and shipwrecks, witches and fairies, curses and clearances, fact and fantasy – the authentic tales in this collection come straight from the heart of a small Highland community. Children and adults alike respond to their timeless appeal. *Tales of the North Coast* were collected in the early 1970s by Alan Temperley and young people at Farr Secondary School in Sutherland. All the stories were gathered from the area between the Kyle of Tongue and Strath Halladale, in scattered communities wonderfully rich in lore that had been passed on by word of mouth down the generations. This wide-ranging selection provides a satisfying balance between intriguing tales of the supernatural and more everyday occurrences. The book also includes chilling eye-witness accounts of the notorious Strathnaver Clearances when tenants were given a few hours to pack up and get out of their homes, which were then burned to the ground.

Out of the Mists

John Barrington

ISBN 1 905222 33 5 PBK £8.99

In the earliest hours of the morning shepherds gather, waiting for the mists that conceal the hillsides to clear. To pass the time they tell tales of roaming giants, marauding monks and weird witches. Enter this world of magic and wonder in *Out of the Mists*, a delightful collection of stories which will captivate and entertain you while answering your questions about Scottish history and folklore.

Why did St Andrew become the patron saint of Scotland?

How can you protect yourself from faerie magic?

What happened to Scotland's last dragon?

John Barrington uses wit and his encyclopaedic knowledge of Scottish folklore to create a compelling collection of stories that will capture the imaginations of readers of all ages.

Bare Feet and Tackety Boots

Archie Cameron

ISBN 0 946487 17 0 PBK £7.95

The last survivor of those who were born and raised on the island of Rum before the First World War tells his story. Factors and schoolmasters, midges and poaching, deer, ducks and McBrayne's steamers; here social history and personal anecdote create a record of a way of life gone not long ago but already almost forgotten. This is the story the gentry couldn't tell.

The authentic breath of the country-wise estate employee.
THE OBSERVER

Rum: Nature's Island

Magnus Magnusson

ISBN 0 946487 32 4 PBK £7.95

Rum: Nature's Island is the fascinating story of a Hebridean island from the earliest times through to the Clearances. It recalls the island in the days it was the sporting playground of a Lancashire industrial magnate, and celebrates its rebirth as a National Nature Reserve, a model for the active ecological management of Scotland's wild places.

Thoroughly researched and written in a lively accessible style, the book includes comprehensive coverage of the island's geology, animals and plants, and people, with a special chapter on the Edwardian extravaganza of Kinloch Castle. There is practical information for visitors to what was once known as the Forbidden Isle; the book provides details of bothy and other accommodation, walks and nature trails. It closes with a positive vision for the island's future: biologically diverse, economically dynamic and ecologically sustainable.

Riddoch on the Outer Hebrides

Lesley Riddoch

ISBN 1 906307 86 5 PBK £12.99

Riddoch on the Outer Hebrides is a thought-provoking commentary based on broadcaster Lesley Riddoch's cycle journey through a beautiful island chain facing seismic cultural and economic change. Her experience is described in a typically affectionate but hard-hitting style; with humour, anecdote and a growing sympathy for islanders tired of living at the margins but wary of closer contact with mainland Scotland.

Let's be proud of standing on the outer edge of a crazy mainstream world – when the centre collapses, the periphery becomes central.
ALISTAIR MCINTOSH

Lewis & Harris: History & Pre-History

Francis Thompson

ISBN 0 946487 77 4 PBK £4.99

The fierce Norsemen, intrepid missionaries and mighty Scottish clans – all have left a visible mark on the landscape of Lewis and Harris. This comprehensive guide explores sites of interest in the Western Isles, from pre-history through to the present day.

Harsh conditions failed to deter invaders from besieging these islands or intrepid travellers from settling, and their legacy has stood the test of time in an array of captivating archaeological remains from the stunningly preserved Carloway Broch, to a number of haunting standing stones, tombs and cairns. With captivating tales – including an intriguing murder mystery and a romantic encounter resulting in dramatic repercussions for warring clans – Francis Thompson introduces us to his homeland and gives us an insight into its forgotten ways of life.

Luath Press Limited

committed to publishing well written books worth reading

LUATH PRESS takes its name from Robert Burns, whose little collie Luath (*Gael.*, swift or nimble) tripped up Jean Armour at a wedding and gave him the chance to speak to the woman who was to be his wife and the abiding love of his life. Burns called one of 'The Twa Dogs' Luath after Cuchullin's hunting dog in Ossian's *Fingal*. Luath Press was established in 1981 in the heart of Burns country, and is now based a few steps up the road from Burns' first lodgings on Edinburgh's Royal Mile.

Luath offers you distinctive writing with a hint of unexpected pleasures.

Most bookshops in the UK, the US, Canada, Australia, New Zealand and parts of Europe either carry our books in stock or can order them for you. To order direct from us, please send a £sterling cheque, postal order, international money order or your credit card details (number, address of cardholder and expiry date) to us at the address below. Please add post and packing as follows: UK – £1.00 per delivery address; overseas surface mail – £2.50 per delivery address; overseas airmail – £3.50 for the first book to each delivery address, plus £1.00 for each additional book by airmail to the same address. If your order is a gift, we will happily enclose your card or message at no extra charge.

ILLUSTRATION: IAN KELLAS

Luath Press Limited
543/2 Castlehill
The Royal Mile
Edinburgh EH1 2ND
Scotland

Telephone: 0131 225 4326 (24 hours)
email: sales@luath.co.uk
Website: www.luath.co.uk